Flights
of Fancy

Flights of Fancy

Marti Aiello

iUniverse, Inc.
Bloomington

FLIGHTS OF FANCY

This is a work of fiction. All of the characters, names, incidents, organizations, and dialogue in this novel are either the products of the author's imagination or are used fictitiously.

iUniverse books may be ordered through booksellers or by contacting:

iUniverse
1663 Liberty Drive
Bloomington, IN 47403
www.iuniverse.com
1-800-Authors (1-800-288-4677)

Because of the dynamic nature of the Internet, any web addresses or links contained in this book may have changed since publication and may no longer be valid. The views expressed in this work are solely those of the author and do not necessarily reflect the views of the publisher, and the publisher hereby disclaims any responsibility for them.

Any people depicted in stock imagery provided by Thinkstock are models, and such images are being used for illustrative purposes only.
Certain stock imagery © Thinkstock.

ISBN: 978-1-4620-4072-8 (pbk)
ISBN: 978-1-4620-4073-5 (ebk)

Printed in the United States of America

iUniverse rev. date: 08/20/2011

Scenes from my childhood flash before me as I look back on eighty years to a time of my life when I enjoyed a freedom to experience of unique and glorious beginning in the hills of West Virginia.

MAUDE and BOBBY JO

A BIRD ON A WIRE

Chapter 1

I stayed with my grandmother for most of my growing up years, while my mother was gone. I never really thought much about it until I grew older and found out that most families had a Mom and Dad at home. But this is about my story and my life, and living in Guerneville, California with my grandma and gramps. The two of them were unique, even oddities among the unique, as I found out much later when I was old enough to figure it out.

He was already old and grizzled when I was barely six years old. I never really knew him but I sure as hell suspected that he was someone special. There was just something exciting about gramps; his blue, sky blue eyes literally sparkled, and he also made my grandma come alive when he looked at her. A pink glow would start at her throat and work itself up to her normally porcelain-like face. You could tell he had her right there, eating out of his palm and ready to laugh, no giggle like a young girl. When I got old enough to know such things as how a guy could turn you on just by looking at you, I knew then how she was really hooked by the old fart; ornery enough to up and die just when he finally got mellow.

My grandmother, Maude, was born on February 9th, 1896, and Bobbie Joe Simpson, "The Human Fly", was born in Ireland in 1896, on a cold, snowy 30th of November, or so he told us. But, you never really knew if he was telling the truth, 'cause that was something rare, my grandmother claimed. They lived all of their lives in California, which goes to say that probably my grandmother wasn't teasing about the veracity of his statement.

Now what I'm going to tell you is the God's truth, cause I ain't no prevaricator like my grandpa was. Just to keep everything on the up and up, the following story was published in the San Francisco Examiner on February 5, 1914. You can look it up, if there is a shred

3

of thinking I might take after 'the ole' fart' as Grammy claimed my grandpa to be.

"Laverna Maude Faylor was married to Bobbie Simpson to the wedding music of the tug and ferry boat whistles and the faint rumbling of truck and electric cars below. Steeple Jack, Bob Simpson and his eighteen years old bride, who calls herself a "Steeple Jill", were married yesterday on the pinnacle of the Ferry Building tower by the Reverend J.M. Heady, "the marrying parson."

Sea gulls wheeled about the lofty altar and bay breezes played with the bride's golden hair as the pair joined hands and answered vows pronounced by the clergyman clinging perilously below them.

A reporter and a photographer of "The Examiner" staff, who were witnesses, hung to the topmost cornice of the tower.

To cap the ceremony, Simpson jumped into his swing at the conclusion of the marriage and pulling himself to the top of the pole and down again.

The plucky bride made the perilous decent waving to the passengers on the ferryboats, and one thousand upturned faces along the Embarcadero.

"I feel like a real sky pilot," said Dr. Heady as he kissed the bride.

In a little room in the interior of the tower behind the four faces of the giant clock, the wedding breakfast was held with sandwiches and cake.

Two months ago a Justice of the Peace married the Simpson couple, but the bride also insisted upon a religious ceremony, and also her desires to be married in the atmosphere in which they work brought about the Ferry Building wedding. Dr. Headly, pastor of the Golden Gate Baptist Church of Oakland is a friend of the pair and readily agreed to officiate.

The Simpson's combined a day of strenuous labor, taking a heavy ball from the top of the Ferry flagpole, guiding it and replacing it. He also painted the flagpole, assisted by his wife, Mrs. Simpson who claims to be the only "Steeple Jill" engaged in the work.

Well, as you can see, even though Bobby Joe was considered less than predictable in relating the truth, because I sure know how to read the facts out of the San Francisco Examiner. He must have told the truth once in a while, especially when he said, "I do," to the preacher, and he never really lied about that until he fell off a pole and got himself killed at thirty-six years of age.

My grandmother wasn't exactly the one to talk about other people's character. She wasn't necessarily what you call an upright virtuous woman herself. As a matter of fact, when my mother up and left me and later my sister Rosie behind, she sure didn't earn herself any points in my book. Besides which, when we got into any trouble at all, my Grammy had the longest arm and the sharpest slap heard in the neighborhood. But all that came later after my cousin, Ralph, fell down the well and got drowned. I guess she must have liked him best, because I'll bet if I as much as fell out of a tree onto a pike, she probably wouldn't have even noticed. I supposed you just can't tell about how a persons' going to act after they get old like Grammy. Like that time that Rosie got a marble stuck up her nose and all she did then was to run her over to the doctor's office and he took out the marble and Rosie got a sucker, which she bragged about and wouldn't even give me a lick. I really don't remember my sister Rosie growing up with my cousins and me. I think I might have been about six years old and suddenly, I woke up one morning and there she was, in bed with Evelyn and me.

The whole Simpson family lived in Guerneville with my great grandparents. My grandmother, Maude, had two daughters from Bobbie Joe, and then there was me and Rosie, Aunt Nora and Uncle Sam, who sometimes lived with us, and also Aunt Frances's three kids, Evelyn, Joe and Clifford, minus Ralph. My great grandmother and grandfather and Aunt Pearl, Grammy's sister, lived on the same property in the small house alongside of the main house and my grandmother Maude ran the whole thing. No doubt about that.

We lived on a farm with a very productive forest of fruit trees and grape vineyards. It was one of few places where the open sun shone on a flat three acres of land. Great Grandfather Faylor had been a farmer in Germany and came up to Redwood country to work in the logging industry. But farming was in his blood and he began to plant peach and apple trees on one acre of his property. Plus my Grammy had a garden of her own where she grew everything we

5

ate. Chicken coops held the laying chickens, and the eggs had to be plucked away from those ornery hens every morning. The rooster blew his bugle everyday, and all of us kids over three years old were put to work doing something, or my Grammy was twisting some ears or pulling hair.

I remember that the winters in Guerneville were cold and wet, and all the girl cousins slept in one bed. My sister, Rosie, and the cousins were all hogging the blankets that Grammy quilted when the old lady came in and booted us out of bed for a breakfast of oatmeal. If we didn't quite hear the first call or understand the command of "time to get yore little fannies out of bed", the next step would be twisting and pulling time. All of us knew that whatever Maude decreed, we needed to obey and to tell the truth at all times. To keep me honest, she would tell me that she would catch a dragonfly and sew my mouth shut if I ever lied. With such a serious injunction implanted in my memory, I always told the truth and spoke my true feelings, even if it hurt. When I went to school and learned from the teacher that all children needed a good eight or nine hours of sleep, I tried to instruct Grammy of that fact. But you can bet she didn't listen to me, and threatened to go down to the school and give that teacher "what for". I decided right there and then, the best thing I could do was get right out of bed when the rooster said so, and avoid turning bald for the time being until I was old enough to leave home and sleep in when I wanted to.

We lived near the Russian River, a tempting walk from our farm that lay outside the town where the trees could hide a small child, and who would know if we really actually got to school on those warm days toward the end of spring and the end of the school year? Sometimes it was just Rosie and me, hoping that Evelyn, Joe or Clifford wouldn't notice if we lagged behind and then split off like a bat out of you know where as we skidded down the slippery slope and ended up on the sandy beach front along the river. Sometimes it was just me and Big Dog who walked us to school everyday then casually lumbered over to the shade of the elm tree where he stretched his long body along the fence until we all came out for recess. Our cousins all seemed dull to Rosie and me. They were just so darn afraid of Grammy catching them at doing anything she wouldn't approve of that it made me wanna puke. Rosie was almost as bad as them. I guess I was just more like my Grampa, who kinda stepped in between Grammy and her switch and me. Not that she ever used it, but it made good sense just to let her whip it around and use up all her energy on scrunching up her face and yelling names like "you little runt, when I catch you I'm gonna whip yore backside where you won't sit down for a week." Grampa would just smile and then take me out for a little walk away from the old witch until she calmed down a bit.

"Come on spout", he'd say, "let's let your Grandma cool off a bit." He would take his big rough hand in mine, and it felt like heaven. His cheeks were always a rosy color and his eyes were the shade of a summer sky. His hair was black and shiny with the pomade he used to slick it down. I never felt as loved or so taken care of as when my grandpa would take me with him and talk 'grownup' like we were friends—close friends.

When I grew older I measured every man I met with the same yardstick as I did with my grandfather, and none ever met his match. I had a small understanding about how it was between him and Grammy, how he could give her that look with a small smile that brought a dimple out on his right cheek, and I would see her change like she'd lost her power to control her world. After he was gone I never saw it again. She ruled with an iron hand and no one on God's green earth could budge her . . . only him and his love. In the spring, the blossoms on the fruit trees scented the whole valley and colored it in shades of light and dark pink, white, and the spring green of new leaves. As the little buds developed into small samples of what it would become full grown, we waited.

It was a time of running barefoot in and out of the rows that lined up like an army, limbs saluting the day and welcoming the sun into the orchards. It was a time when even Maude was in as good a mood as was possible for the likes of an ill conceived old biddy like her. As long as we kids kept as far away as possible and did our chores in a timely fashion, she left us alone. We never knew whether she was mad, sad, or disgusted, she just registered mean whenever we glanced her way. I don't ever recall her lips curving upward even a little bit after Grampa got him self killed. I think at one time, she must have been a beauty as seen in the photos that were scattered around the parlor. Maybe she wasn't the smiling type because the mouth only showed full lips in a pout and her gray eyes arched in a question. A younger version of Maude at about eight years old showed the same firm jaw-line, steely eyes full of herself with a back

7

rim-rod strait as a an arrow. No one could doubt the image of a future dictator who ruled all within her realm. In the years when I lived with my grandma she had that sameness of character that held you in abeyance.

When the summer drew into fullness and the fruit trees became ready for harvest Grammy employed a steady crew at hand for the picking. She chose the day carefully, and as with the rest of everything that came within the realm of Maude Simpson's control. We stood ready with buckets and baskets in hand, waiting for the orders. She led her troops into the rows of heavy limbs weighted down with fruit. Young and old, arms and necks reddened from the sun, reached for the fruits with faces upturned, then necks bent toward the buckets in a repetitive motion that continued throughout the morning. Buckets of fresh water and dippers were available, but carefully watched by Grammy when the trips toward the bucket became too frequent. Her eyes would tell you when and how long to linger.

Maude dressed in overalls and was not averse to climbing the trees to reach the fruit with a basket-like retriever that pulled the cots or peaches off the limbs. Her industry never wavered and hours would pass without a pause as she feverishly worked to strip every tree of its bounty. Who could slack off or draw back from giving over as much energy as this old woman who led her minions with a determination that bespoke almost a frantic level of commitment to work as long as the daylight hours permitted? When the day did end, it was Maude who washed up at the outside faucet. Then she changed into her long cotton dress, put a clean apron on and began cooking, preparing vegetables and meat for a pot of stew, all the while directing her brood of kids and grand kids to clean up and set the table. Weary dirt and sweat-streaked faces had to be cleaned, and hair needed to be combed, before sitting down at table to eat the late dinner. It was the only time that elbows holding up a weary head could be overlooked. For a time all was silent as food was shoveled into the mouth without enthusiasm and eyes seemed to want to close without intent.

It was only Maude who remained upright at the table with all her family bent on just getting through a meal and then to bed. She did not ask for help in cleaning up after dinner, and when we awoke at daybreak, it was to a table set with dishes and cutlery and bowls of oatmeal steaming hot and ready to be inhaled as quick as the spoon could reach the mouth. It was the first day of picking the orchard on the west side of our farm. Grammy announced that the one who would pick the most fruit before the day's end would receive one dollar. Our ears perked up, faces became more animated and even a smile or two appeared on the faces of the younger ones around the table. We were eager to finish our breakfast and begin another day.

Great Grandma and Grandpa Faylor worked together in the packing shed, carefully selecting each piece of fruit, eyeing them for damage and covering each one with a square of green tissue before lining them up in the wooden crates. If Grandpa were not on a job in the City, he would be loading the crates onto the truck and delivering them to the stores. Otherwise, at the end of the Grump's workday, he spent evenings loading up the trucks for the long drive into San Francisco. Once in a while he'd sneak me into the front seat and take me along for the ride. I would get to stay the whole day with him. Me, tucked away somewhere in the building he was working on, or watching him climb the steeple of a church or some such job that he was asked to do. "Do you want me to teach you the trade, Princess?"

"No thanks, Gramps, I'll just watch." He'd grin and push his hat to the back of his head.

"Smart kid," he'd agree, and off he would go.

Chapter 2

It was another one of those rare days that Gramps took me out of harms way of Grammy, who woke up especially critical of everybody and everything she laid those steely gray eyes on. The rest of the kids had scattered right after breakfast on a Saturday morning. Grandma and Grandpa Faylor left the main house right after Maude broke a dish over my head when I spilt a glass of milk. That's when Gramps took charge and tried to subdue his wild mate. "Git in the car kitten, you can come to work with me today." You'd have to know I cleared out of the room in record time. My head hurt a little from the noggin' bashing but that was nothing compared to a holiday with Gramps.

By the time gramps got behind the steering wheel, my head was feeling just fine and the incident with Grammy was forgotten in the surprise turnabout that resulted in a day with my favorite person in the whole wide world. The car was big black Buick, built like a tank, with a wide front and plenty of chrome shinning in the morning sun. I rolled the window down and put my head to the side to catch the wind as we whizzed by the orchards on our way out of town. I wasn't about to waste a single second thinking about what happened, but determined to get the most out of the bonus day with someone I loved so much. Gramps cleared his throat and spit out of the window before he spoke. "Your grandma wasn't always such a hard woman Lynette, she's just tired of all the responsibility of taking care of everybody and everything. Your Mother got herself in trouble when she was only fourteen, and you and Rosie ended up on our doorstep. The same thing happened to your Aunt Frances too, and she left your cousins with the family and took off, and we haven't seen either one of them since." He paused. "Well, Frances did come back and took her kids for a little while when she married that butcher down in Richmond."

It was the first time anyone had mentioned us having a real mother and I sat there in shock. "What's my mother's name?"

"It's Rosemary."

"Is she gonna come back and take us away from you and Grammy?"

"Well, that would be over my dead body, honey. I'm not gonna let anybody take my favorite girl away."

With that he reached over and patted me on the shoulder. "Don't your worry your pretty little head over anything. You know what I'm gonna do Lynette?"

I shook my head. "What are you gonna do Gramps?"

"When we finish on my job this afternoon. I'm gonna buy you a two-wheeler . . . a blue one."

I swallowed hard, me on a two-wheel bike riding down the hill to school come September. I couldn't believe it. "I love you Gramps." I moved away from the window and snuggled closer to my grandpa, the best in the whole wide world. The closer we got to the ferry slip, the more excited I became. Gramps pulled onto the ferry at Benicia, and we settled in for a long trip across the bay to San Francisco. "Where are we going to buy the bike?" I asked.

"Well, you just leave that up to your old Grandpa. I have a man who has all kinds of things he's picked up. If we can find a blue bicycle, then we'll buy it. But, if he can't come up with a blue one, could you settle for something like red?

"Course, I would. Any color is all right with me. You're the best grandpa I could ever have." I looked at him in profile and decided he was next to God in my estimation.

When we got over to San Francisco, Gramps called the man who had 'all kinds of things', and left me in charge of 'his business' and off he went in a truck that was parked inside of the building. We were at a big warehouse of some kind, and there wasn't much to do but hang around until he got back. It was about noon, and I was

11

getting kinda hungry when he finally came back. In the back of the truck he had borrowed was a bike wheel sticking out from under a canvas covering that gramps always carried along in the truck. He hopped on to the back of the truck, and flipped the covering off like a magician showing his tricks, and there it was, the prettiest red bike I had ever seen.

"Gramps, it's just the color I wanted. Could I ride it around?"

"Do you know how to ride a bike?"

"Well, no, but it don't take no genius to pedal a bike, does it?"

"Nope, I guess it don't. Git yourself on it, and take 'er out."

Well, I did attempt to mount the bike, but I could only stand on one pedal and attempt to push it along with the other foot. When I tried both pedals, the bike went wobbly and skidded out from under me and I ended up with skinned shins and a bruise on my knee.

"I think we better wait until we git home and you can practice on the dirt path. Don't worry it jes' takes a little gittin' use to. You'll have it mastered in no time a' tall."

My Grandpa had to go to work, so he set me up in a little room and handed me some papers to draw on and went out the door. I had the whole day to work on getting me up on that bike and learning how to maneuver that thing around until I had it licked. By the time gramps got back, I met him at the door to the warehouse, riding my bike like I was born to the saddle.

Gramps was so proud of me! In less than a day, I had learned the hard way, I must confess. I had more bruises and scrapes than you could shake a stick at, but I learned good.

We had to change vehicles and put the bike in the trunk of the Buick. It was seven o'clock when we got back to Guerneville, and when we rolled into the yard and I showed off the new bicycle. It was like sudden lighting in the sky on a clear day. My Grandmother hit the roof. "You crazy old man, you're gonna git that girl killed. What were you thinking of? Now you take that thing back where you got it, Bobbie, I'm not gonna stay home worrying every time she goes out the door."

"Now Maude, you can't be coddling these kids the rest of their lives."

"Well, you don't have a damn thing to say how I raise these kids. You know I would never have approved of your taking a free hand in having one of them get hurt, maybe be crippled for the rest of their lives. Just look at her, she's got more bruises and cuts than I can count. You put that bike away, and I don't want to see any of 'em riding it until they get old enough to handle it." Grammy stormed out the door, slamming it so hard she liked to pull the hinges loose.

Gramps rubbed his whiskered chin and took off down the hill, the tires on the truck spitting dirt and cinders as he gunned the motor as fast as that old Ford would go. Now, what was so aggravating to everybody who knew my Grandmother was that her own life as a young girl was so contrary to what she expected form us. Grandmother Faylor told me tales of how Grammy would never follow the rules she set up for her grandchildren. "She was a wild on, never stayed still, taking off lickety-split whenever the mood struck her. She did pretty much whatever she pleased. Wouldn't listen to a word I said."

It was true what Grandmother Faylor said. Maude would never let us climb trees and everyone, including me, was afraid of heights for as long as we lived. I learned later that Maude not only worked with gramps, climbing poles and even did the most outrageous thing no one else would do if they were in their right mind. She did all kinds of daredevil stunts with my grandpa, such as walking the wings of an airplane in flight and dangling in mid-air below the plane, clutching a cable in her teeth. Bobbie Joe and Maude lived life on the edge working at times performing stunts as advertisements for movies and such. I know this is really hard to swallow. I wouldn't have believed it myself, except their shenanigans hit the newspapers and made history.

My Grandmother, Maude, never talked about her life and the way she had lived in her youth. She would never let us kids climb, or be subject to any activity that might be a hazard. Yet she climbed the trees to pick the fruit, climbed up rickety ladders to fix the roof, all

13

the while warning us to be careful lest we get hurt. I never realized what an unusual childhood I had lived. I think, had I not had her as a parent figure, I probably would have been more courageous in the sort of life I chose for myself.

Grammy never ceased to amaze me. Every once in a while, she'd pack all of us kids in the old Buick, along with a wicker basket full of sandwiches, fruit, a jug of lemonade, and water, and off we'd go through Duncan Mills on to the beach at Jenner-by-the Sea or Bodega Bay. I never saw my grandmother smoke or drink while she was at home in Guerneville, but when she got out of the house and a thousand miles away in her head, she would climb up the hill and sit on a rock so she could watch us. While she was sitting on that big rock, she'd pull out a pack of cigarettes, light up, and sit there, drinking bear or coca cola and smiling. As long as we kids didn't get into trouble that day, she could even laugh and tease. It was as though she put the old Grammy out and brought in this strange woman who inhabited her body for a time. Even the youngest kid in the clan knew enough not to rock the boat. Every one of us understood that this was just a temporary grandma whose wonderfulness was an apparition that wasn't supposed to last.

The memories of the occasional days spent at the beach had to last for a long time. Just because, like measles, mumps or chicken pox, when Grammy tended to us with a gentle compassionate hand, it had a limited course to run and you better get used to it. I guess I never described my grandmother in detail so you could get a true picture of her. She had a chin that preceded the rest of her body. It stuck out like the pugilist you might see in the boxing ring when he'd already won the fight. The rest of her face sort of just laid back and watched the chin do all the work. The eyes were normally set at half-mast, just waiting for somebody to misstep. Then those steely gray eyes would narrow down to slits, shooting out darts that would penetrate the toughest of skin. They spoke a language all their own. Sometimes saying, 'that's one, and the next move might be your last.' Other times, you could already feel your blistered behind throbbing with the licking you were about to receive.

The amazing thing was that teacher, neighbor, or whomever you talked to in the whole Napa Valley County pointed to the Simpson family as the 'best trained kids in Guerneville.' Now, that was just on the surface, all of us Simpson's were absolutely genius in getting away with murder. Our spotless reputation was never questioned as we registered faces of innocent benevolence. We had all become actors of a sort. Capable of falling into the role of whatever part we were expected to play. Every emotion could be displayed before the public and a flawless performance could win the day. By the time I had reached puberty, I realized that we all had followed the example that our beloved Grandpa, Bobbie Jo, had set before us. You never challenged Grammy you simply kept quiet and followed your own path.

Thinking back, I believe we may have inherited the best of our role models. Each one of the children, reared under the direction of Maude and Bobbie Jo, became a relentless worker who never quit and never sidestepped trouble until it hit head on. We knew when it was time to stay and when to walk away and never look back. Our parents had learned that piece of wisdom at an early age when my mother and aunts decided to leave the protection of the dictator in charge, and struck out on their own to begin a life on their own terms. The biggest mistake they made though, was to desert their own kids. Rosie and me were too young to remember, and maybe that was a good thing. You can't cry over what you don't have. It was good to know about mothers though, in case somebody asked. I could always say, 'I never knew her', and let somebody else figure it out.

Some memories I have of my Grammy are strange, but wonderful; the times when she put on her riding pants and hiking boots and took us kids to the Armstrong Woods Park. She packed a picnic lunch with the jars of fruit she had canned and apples and peaches galore. Fried chicken or roast and her homemade bread was wrapped in a table clothe kept for these special occasions. All of the kids squeezed into the black Buick, overlapping until you couldn't tell whose hand, foot or elbow belonged to whom. My grandmother Maude turned into a young girl. She would promise something special for the first one of us who could get up to the highest hill before she did. There was always lots of scrambling, slipping and sliding in the loose black dirt, covered with fallen leaves a foot deep. At times we would see a coyote staring back at us before he took off like a bat out of hell when we came too close. Squirrels and woodland creatures scurried about as we made our way up the hill on a worn path or blazed a new trail in our race to the top. When the last of our brood finally reached the pinnacle, Maude would be sitting there having a smoke and drinking coca cola. Funny though, she never smoked a cigarette except when we had our special trips to the hills above Guerneville or at the ocean beach at Jenner or Bodega Bay. In my mind when I look back, I would see a younger Maude, slim waist and hips filling out the riding britches quite well. She would usually wear an old tattered wool sweater when we went to the beach. It seemed as if she shed her dresses along with a hurried, impatient and cranky old lady when she pulled on her pants and that old wool sweater. She became a funny, younger woman whose friendliness infected anyone who had come along. There was much laughter and teasing, running and chasing along the rocks and an occasional fall into the water that did not upset her at all. It was glorious.

When we started out and when we returned home, Grammy taught us old songs that she had learned when she was a child. Her deep husky voice joining with the tenor and soprano voices of all of us blended well into a serious choir. The upright piano at home had provided the background for any who had a proclivity for learning the keyboard. It was one thing she never minded when we played a musical piece over and over until it would have driven the rest out of the house. When Maude declared a holiday, she was as dedicated to having a good time as anyone. It seemed so special to us because in our short childhood, it also seemed so rare by comparison. When I became an adult, I was able to understand the contrasts that seemed so radical in the mind of a child.

When my grandfather came along, the trips were twice as much fun for me. It wasn't as often of course, because gramps had much to do on the weekends. Maude always drove the big black Buick. Gramps taught her when she was fourteen years old. He took her out in his old Ford V8 and they traveled the back roads in the evening after the logging trucks were finished for the day. Gramps said that Grammy was the best driver he was acquainted with. She'd tear around the bends in the road without missing a beat. Keeping the car steady, and was as good on the hills as she was on the highway. Gramps taught me too, and he claimed the same about me. He started with me on his lap, guiding the steering wheel when I was very young, maybe six or seven years old. By the time I was ten, I had pretty good control over the vehicle, whether it was the old Ford truck or the one at the warehouse in San Francisco. He'd let me take the truck around the inside, driving real slow and easy. I promised I would never drive unless he was present. And I kept my word.

My grandfather was as good as a carpenter when it came to fixing things up. When the regular upkeep of our old house needed attention, the plumbing stopped up in the kitchen or a bathroom toilet and had to be unstopped, he was right there. Rooms needed painting, roofs needed shingles and then there was work to be done on the old Faylor house. Maude's elderly parents had similar repairs to be made. Supplies from the hardware stores were picked up and brought home in the old truck on Saturday and Bobbie Joe's work had been laid out for him on those weekends. Much of the time, Maude and Bobbie Joe worked together on the projects, but it was the rare weekends that were set aside for the best of times in my memories of childhood on the ranch in the summer. Especially when we traveled over the back roads to the rocky beach of Bodega Bay.

Chapter 3

Grammy never talked much about her childhood or the time spent with gramps before me and Rosie and our cousins moved in. It was gramps and his gift for telling stories of the "good ol' days" that I learned of his early years before and after he was married to Maude. She was only fifteen when they got married, and he said, "She fell for me like a ton of bricks." I could believe it too. Gramps was something special.

He would begin with, "when your grandmother and me were young that woman was dynamite. Never missed a beat when I asked her to join me when I put on the rigging that strapped us to the telephone pole or a smoke stack for a repair job at the top. I tell you she was fearless. She'd pull on a pair of my old pants and shirt and shimmy up that pole like she was born to it. She pinned her hair back and put on a cap and you couldn't tell her from any other steeple Jack working the trade. Honey, she was something to see. One time her cap blew off, and her hair went wild under the stiff wind up there, the hairpins came out and her long, honey-colored hair blew around her face like the head of an overripe dandelion. I got really scared that she wouldn't be able see and misstep somehow. But not my Maude, she just leaned back against the rigging and commenced to braid the hair into two long plaits, twisting the end pieces into a knot and tied them off." Bobby Joe hesitated, shaking his head from side to side. You could tell he was real proud of Grammy.

"Not many women like your grandmother. No sir! She's one of a kind."

"Tell me more, gramps. I like the stories about when you and Grammy were young."

"Well, now, I betcha she didn't tell you about the time me and her were doing some work for the circus, did she?"

"No, grandpa. I told ya' she didn't talk of anything you or she did when you were young. Every time I'd ask, she'd just say, 'run along' and don't bother me with all that tripe.'"

"Well, maybe she just might not wanna remember how it was between me and her. But your grandma was hell on wheels when she was young. But don't you go repeating what we talk about sprout. I don't want to get into trouble with that old woman. She can take the foam off a perfectly good mug of beer just by looking at it. I actually saw it happen once."

"Well, what about the circus story gramps, what happened when you joined the circus?"

"No, Lynette. We didn't join the circus. We just performed at the circus on the weekends. I knew this pilot that had this airplane. It was one of the older planes, built back in the 1918, called a Curtiss "Jenny". Actually Howard Hughes flew one of 'em around the world . . . it took three days. Anyway, a guy I knew who was a pilot asked me and Maude if we wanted to do some 'stunts'. Sure, I tell him. Well, he took us up a few times to get used to him doing some acrobatics, figure eights, loops and rolls. Well, I'll be damned if Maude didn't just love the stuff we were doing and asked if maybe we could do some tricks out on the wings. The plane had double wings and the guy, you know, the pilot said he could hook us to a heavy-duty wire and we could suspend from the wire. We'd wear a 'chute, so if we fell, we'd just glide down like a snow flake landing on a pine tree."

"Were you scared, gramps?"

"Not a lick. And neither was your grandmother. In fact, I think I was more scared than she was. And one more thing."

By that time, my eyes must have looked as big as saucers; I couldn't believe the fun they had before they got married. I told gramps so. "What was that?" I asked.

"Your grandmother was three months pregnant with your mother, Rosemary.

"So, I got a chance to go up in the airplane too."

"Well, no. You weren't born yet, you had to wait a few years until you were hatched."

Wow! I can't wait to tell Rosie."

"You can't do that Lynette."

"Why not, gramps?"

"Cause it's not proper to be caught having a baby when you're not married. You keep that in mind, honey."

"Okay, Gramps." I didn't think that was such a big deal, but I didn't say so.

It was one of those damnably hot days in Guerneville when the breeze that usually blew off the river and cooled the town around five o'clock in the afternoon just quit. Maybe, like the rest of us, it lost interest toward the end of summer. We had finished with the fruit picking, and it was between the time when the grapes were coming into their fullness, but wasn't quite ready to be harvested. Grammy had finished up with the canning, and the apple trees wouldn't be ready for a month or two. It was a time to lay back and relax a little. Energy kind of leaked out of everything that had a heart. Even 'Big Dog' lay around almost not caring a lick if one of the kids sat on him or about the flies whizzing around his ears. He just didn't have enough energy to wag his tail in exasperation. Even a walk down to the river had lost its attraction. Just to liven up the day, my cousin Clifford had built a tree house unbeknownst to Grammy, and the first thing the little turd did was to fall out of the tree. Clifford was always a little dumb in my estimation, and if he had the brains of a gnat, he would have known not to cry out loud if he wanted to keep playing in that tree house. But, like I said, this kid was dumb as a nail, and started wailing like he'd broken a bone or something. Of course, out comes 'Mad Maude', cursing and threatening to lock all of us up in the shed and throw away the key. She claimed it was the only way to keep us out of trouble.

My other cousins were all gathered around their brother as he laid himself out like a corpse and whimpered like he was on his deathbed. Evelyn and Joe stood there like it was their place to mourn the passing of a close relative. For Pete's sake, we could have had a lot of fun playing Tarzan and the Apes if that little dummy had kept quiet. I mean, geez, we only had a few weeks to go before school started, and he had to go and ruin it. Me and Rosie just stood there looking pitiful like we really felt sorry about Clifford's 'accident'. Well Grammy didn't lock us up or anything, not even a threat to give us all a beating. I figured it was because me and Rosie saved the day by looking down at Clifford as we allowed a tear to run down our cheeks, just like Shirley Temple did in one of the movies we saw at the Rivertown Theater. I got to thinkin' about it later and I told Rosie that I thought we ought to go to Hollywood and be a star in the movies. I could be another Shirley Temple and she could be Jane Withers. I could have a career and earn lots of money and be famous. Rosie and me spent the next few weeks before school started, planning how to make enough money to buy a ticket for a bus ride down to Los Angeles. I picked up a map of California and put our marks on Hollywood. Now we had to figure out where we could go to work to earn enough to buy the tickets and how long it would take to save up for the trip. By the time September rolled around, schoolwork and chores almost erased the plans we had to change our names. I was going to be Jennifer and Rosie was Lynda, the Crawford girls. For nearly a month, we talked about the trip to Hollywood after school and talked some more in bed before falling asleep. On Saturdays we hung around the theater down on Second Street, and begged the guy to who put up the 'Coming Attractions 'signs to give them to us rather that throw them away, then rolled up the frayed posters and hid them under the bed. By the time November rolled around, we had collected about twenty or thirty posters, then we sat for hours talking about Mickey Rooney, Judy Garland and Deana Durbin and others that I can't recall now. By the end of November, our thoughts shifted to Christmas trees and presents. Then slowly, our dreams for a career as famous movie stars drifted away like a big red balloon that you buy at a carnival, that either loses it air or sails away on a summer breeze.

Grammy had bought a little turkey and stuck him in the chicken coop to fatten up for a Thanksgiving Day dinner. All of us were bored with chickens. They just pecked around in the yard and flew up on the fences and pooped wherever they wanted. But now we had a turkey. His name was Ralph, after my cousin who had died. But we called him "Alfie", so as not to upset Grammy. He had this red necktie thing hanging down the front of his chest, and he was much more interesting than the chickens. As soon as we came home from

21

school, the first thing we would do is go to the henhouse to check up on Alfie. Grammy had given us the job of fattening him up for the upcoming dinner. Rosie and me chased him around and around until we could catch him and then we'd hold his head down to eat the bowl of feed. It would take about an hour to round him up as he ran from the hen house out into the orchard, through the vineyard and back to the henhouse where he would fly up to the rafters and hang out for a while. It was a lot of work for Rosie and me, but we had been given a job to do and we had always been taught to do the best we could at every task at hand.

It was only a week before Thanksgiving Day and Alfie hadn't gained a pound. He was just about the same weight as when he came to live with us, only very nervous when you got close to him. So Grandpa had to go out and buy a turkey from the store. He said, 'it probably was a defected bird' since me and Rosie had told him how much time we had spent trying to get him to eat right. We just gave up and by Christmas, that turkey had gained about twenty pounds. Alfie was now smothered in gravy and we gave thanks, and everybody was blessed to partake of this meal.

During the time between Christmas and a two-week vacation from school, I spent more time going to work with my Grandpa. This was a magical time learning more about his "side-businesses". It should be pointed out that I was born at the time of Prohibition. Bobbie Joe had been involved in running a distillery inside the old warehouse down near Fishermen's Wharf. He told me that he used to supply the liquor for all the nightclubs in San Francisco. He paid off the 'cops' to turn a blind eye to his business. It was during this period that Bobbie Joe was able to 'up' his income and put a little aside for the future. But, it was a secret that I was not to talk about to Maude.

"You've got to promise me that you won't say anything about what happens here to your Grandmother."

I crossed my heart three times. "I won't tell Grandma anything, ever."

"Good girl," he said as he picked me up and hugged me hard. That was the first secret that I carried in my heart for many years. The second one was that a blond-haired woman called "Sally" would come and visit with Grandpa after one of his jobs was over. She was all 'gussied' up in fancy clothes and a white fur stole over her shoulder. "Sally, this is my grand daughter, Lynette Diane Simpson."

"I'm pleased to meet you Lynette. I hope we can be good friends."

I stuttered and shook her hand. She wore bright red nail polish on long nails that turned down at the ends. I swore right there that when I got older, I would grow long nails and paint them red just like Sally's. She had full lips that matched her nail polish and when she smiled, her teeth were white and shiny.

Grandpa took on a whole new character when she was around. He joked and laughed a lot. Her eyes were shining when he complimented her dress and good looks. I didn't know what to make of this. I'd never seen this side of him. He was like a rooster in a hen house. Struttin' around and showing off like a peacock was not his usual style. Sometimes, he would take off with her in a white convertible car and would not come back until late. But when he did, he always brought me a nice dinner and a toy of some kind. Most of the time I didn't think anything about it, and Sally brought me chocolates from Ghiradelli's when she came visiting after that first time. Grandpa told me she was a dancer and performed on stage in a big theater. He laughed when I asked him if I could go with him sometime to see her. "Not likely to happen, sprout, that kind of entertainment is only for grownups."

I was true to my word and never told anyone what went on when I took my trips with Gramps . . . and I never told the secrets until many years after I grew up and moved away. By that time he had died and it just didn't seem important anymore.

The Christmas vacation ended and I went back to school, and the meeting with a woman named, "Sally", became a lost memory until years later when I had grown up and moved away from Guerneville. School began to take up most of my day and evenings doing homework. A few extra days off from school came along when we had the Russian River flooding over the bridge that connected the town on Route 116 leading out of Guerneville. It had rained for six days straight and the river was rising inches at a time. It hadn't crested yet, but our trees were already dipping their roots and water was coming from the river to a point where we needed to wear our galoshes and rubber boots up to our knees. It was always an exciting time when the flood waters would cause schools to close and boats on the river would be unable to be rowed back to shore because of the swift currents taking it far off its destination. It's owners both frightened and excited by power of the rushing river.

Despite the inconvenience, everybody you talked to exhibited high spirits by the disaster that might flood their basements or cause them to be confined to their homes. Car motors were shorted out by damp wires while driving through the flooded streets, stranding the occupants in odd places without a nearby telephone. Clusters of people you wouldn't ordinarily talk to gathered together and complained to one another about in a town where with the river threatening their livelihood or property. Whatever the problems engendered by these rather frequent events, when the flood had done its damage the streets were cleared of fallen trees and litter and from the residue of the muddy aftermath, not one resident moved away because of the floods. Neighbors helped clean the public places like schools, libraries and the mess left behind, but still, they survived and thrived in this small haven they loved so dearly.

The best thing about floods though, when I think about it, was that the whole town changed us all for a time. When we went down to the grocery store, we stopped and talked to the people who had lost their boats or to businessmen with lost merchandise. Clothes and household furnishing were offered to those whose ruined homes would need repair work done, and replacement of the necessities to start over. My Grandfather offered the loan of tools and help on his days off. Grandmother Maude parted with some of the chickens and a whole lot of her canned goods to the folks who were in need. It was a giving time, and everyone profited by the largess of some, and the lifelong friendship of others who received the bounty of lasting appreciation.

One little girl just four years old had been separated from the family and after hours of searching by her family, she was not found. The news went out to the community. Neighbors alerted everyone they knew and the whole town showed up within a short time. It was late afternoon when the search began and the consensus of many was that she had been drowned. By evening, flashlights were brought out and women gathered at the schoolhouse with hot food for the men who had tramped along the river or around the hills for hours. One team of men would come back to eat and drink coffee while another team continued to scour the area. Prayers and belief in their efforts were rewarded when the little girl was found in the backyard playhouse on Neely Road. When she was brought back to her family, the whole town celebrated like it was the Fourth of July. Shotguns popping firepower brought the search parties back to the schoolhouse, tired and spent, but with grateful hearts that their efforts had been worth the trouble.

Chapter 4

It was near the end of my fourth grade. I had just turned ten years old and developed a crush on Danny Newcastle. He was a little shorter than me, but he had such a nice smile, and I melted every time he looked my way. I think he liked me too, but when he was with other boys, he wouldn't even look at me. In the schoolyard, Danny would hang around with the guys, and throw paper missiles at the girls, not necessarily aimed at me, but to any girl. When I wasn't with him, I was thinking about him. I told my girlfriend, Jenny, just how much I liked Danny. Like a ninny, she told him. I was so embarrassed, I couldn't look at him, and when he looked my way, I turned beet-red. The next day, during recess, Danny ran up behind me and pulled my hair. Jenny came over and took my arm and whispered in my ear, "I think he likes you Lynette."

"No, he doesn't, he hurt my head when he did that."

"That's because he likes you."

I picked up a piece of gravel from the ground and threw it at Danny's head. He was so mad he returned the favor. 'This wasn't going the way it should,' I thought.

"Lynette, why did you do that?" Jenny rolled her eyes and walked over to a group of girls who had seen me throw the stone, and they all looked at me and laughed.

The bell rang and recess was over. I felt so confused I went into the bathroom and cried. I couldn't go back to class with my nose running and my eyes red, so I went home. Grandpa came home early that day and was leaning over the raised hood of the old Ford when I came back from school. I told him what had happened and he just laughed.

"You've got a lot to learn, Lynette. I think you'd better just forget about Danny, and wait a few years before you let yourself start running after boys. Now, ask your grandmother to fix us a pitcher of lemonade and we can have a little talk."

Grammy made the lemonade, but when it came to talking about my episode with Danny, she said she didn't have time for such foolishness and went out into the yard and started taking the wash off the line. She brought the laundry basket into the house.

"At long as you're home, you can fold the towels and sheets. Get the sprinkling bottle out to dampen the clothes to be ironed, and tell that old man out there to finish working on the truck and then get washed up."

I never did find out what went wrong with me and Danny Newcastle who stayed as far away from me as he could from that day on. It wasn't the only time that I embarrassed myself and wanted to go hole up in a cave for the rest of my life. This other time that I recall was when I was almost eleven years old, and this kid, Daryl Dudley Holymeyr, was fourteen years old. Daryl did not attend public school, but stayed in a boarding school and attended St. Thomas Aquinas School for Boys in Santa Rosa. He came home for a three-week period in the summer and rarely mixed with the town kids. We met when I bumped into him on one of my frequent hikes in the hills above Armstrong Woods. We introduced ourselves and we walked together for a couple of miles, sharing stories about our lives. I felt a little out of my league. He was so much more grownup than I, though I pretended to be from one of the old families of Guerneville, owning acres of property left by my great grandparents. I told him I was thirteen, going on fourteen. Only a little of that was true and I would bet my socks, I'd never be found out.

I promised to meet Dudley the following day and we hiked again. I stole some of the fried chicken out of the icebox and fixed up a nice lunch for us. We ate the chicken and the fruit that I brought along and then laid down on the tablecloth we used for picnics. He began to kiss me. We kissed for a long time; then Dudley raised himself and leaned on his arm as he reached across my chest to touch the small budding bust that had just begun to swell. I let him. Laying there and waiting for the next step, he put his leg across mine and began to wriggle like a snake. It felt interesting, but I didn't

27

know what I was supposed to be doing, so I just lay there. When he reached up my dress and pulled at my pants, I reacted. "What are you doing?" I asked.

"I just wanted to touch you," he hesitated. "Down there."

"I thought you went to a Catholic school."

"I do."

"Don't you believe in God?"

"What's that got to do with anything?"

"My Grandmother said that God would strike me dead if I let a boy touch me there."

"It won't happen."

"How do you know?"

"Let me try it."

"If God doesn't strike me dead, my grandma might."

Not wanting to test Him or Her, I decided it was time to go home. By the end of our conversation, we packed up the leftovers and rolled them up in the tablecloth and headed back down the hill. We didn't talk much and Daryl went his way and I went mine. I thought back a year when we were on summer vacation from school. It was one of those hot early evenings after we had eaten our dinner. We had stripped down to our pants or shorts and were taking turns squirting the hose at one another. All the kids were running around not really trying to escape the sudden burst of water and screaming with pleasure when we caught the blast of cold contact with our almost naked bodies. Later on we toweled off and sat shivering in the night air as we snuggled close to Grandpa on the large canvas glider swing.

I was looking down at my chest and one side had developed a swelling. "Look Grandpa, I must have got a skeeter bite."

"Go and show it to your grandmother. I think it might be more than a mosquito."

I ran in and told grandma what grandpa had said, thinking she'd get the all-purpose salve out and use it on my chest.

"How old are you now, Lynette Diane?

"Ten going on eleven, Grandma."

"Well, looks like you're getting ready to grow up." I thought then what 'growing' up might mean in terms of what I might be entitled to. Maybe it was all right to lay down with Dudley Holymeyr, but I had a pretty good hunch, I shouldn't ask. Anything that felt that good must be a sin, and anyone with Holy in his name does not necessarily mean he is.

Chapter 5

In 1938, two momentous events happened that changed the course of my life and the lives of everyone in the Simpson family. My favorite person in the whole world, my grandfather, Bobbie Joe, fell from a hundred and thirty foot high perch. He was replacing a missing brass cap on the top of the pole coming off the smokestack where the old red, white and blue flapped around in the wind, proudly shimmering in the air high above the city of San Francisco. By chance, his image was caught on film when a tourist snapped the picture of my gramps as he fell to his death. The newspaper described his body as being mangled beyond recognition. This explained the two-day period when Gramps had been missing and grandma threatened to kill the son of a bitch when he came home. Though he had never done anything like this before, he was guilty of imbibing a little too much of ole' Jim Beam, and sometimes dragging himself out of the Buick and teetering up to the house and singing "I'll take you home again, Kathleen. Across the ocean wide and wild." This is what Grammy expected, not the news brought by a man in a dark blue serge suit and shiny black shoes.

When the Company boss had come up to Guerneville to break the news to Grammy, she had been madder than a wet hen for two days, and it was hard to make the adjustment from mad to sad. After pacing up and down out in the yard, muttering to herself, she finally came into the house and shook the man's hand after he had explained that the company would take care of all the funeral expenses and see about getting some cash money to her as well. The week following Gramps death was full of activity. People were coming and going. The neighbors brought food wrapped in a dishcloth and offering whatever the folk might need.

The body of my grandfather was brought back to Guerneville and the casket was set up in the parlor that we never used. It was a small room, always meticulously cared for, with dark wine-colored velvet drapes hanging in the windows that were never opened. Neighbors came and set in the straight back chairs that were rarely used except for relatives visiting infrequently at holidays. The lights were dim and people whispered to one another. Mostly we kids were kept dressed in our very best clothes for three days and told to keep quiet.

The last day, a large black hearse parked out front and we followed it up to the cemetery where the burial took place. The Simpson family had their own special place under a large tree spreading its branches almost all over the number of head stones beneath it. I looked over the crowd of people surrounding the casket. Away from the people, I noticed a tall woman with platinum blond hair, not made up like I had seen her years ago, but in a black two-piece suit with a ruffled white blouse. She stood alone, not moving. I thought I saw a small smile on her face. Though I couldn't swear that it was my grandfather's old girl friend, because she wore no lipstick or rouge as I remembered. But I wondered at the time if it might be her. After the casket was lowered into the ground, the woman left and we all went home and had a feast that went on for another three hours.

The cemetery was a wonderful place for me. I could go as often as I wanted to visit my grandfather. The dirt path was lined with big trees that met overhead, leaning toward the opposite side like they were whispering together. It formed some sort of a tunnel and the number of trees that lined the pathway didn't allow a lot of sunlight to penetrate. After a few months of having this brooding place to myself, I began to bring my cousins and some of my very close friends with me. We'd play hide and go seek between the cemetery plots, teetering on the short cement enclosures that outlined the places where the tombstones were placed. It became our new playground. Charlotta Kraigbaum taught us a really creepy song called "The worms crawl in and the worms crawl out," and it went like this,

"Did you ever think, as a hearse goes by/that you might be the next to die?

They wrap you up in a big white sheet/ and bury you down about six foot deep.

They put you in a big black box/ and cover you up with dirt and rocks

31

And all goes well for about a week/ and then the coffin begins to leak."

"The worms crawl in and the worms crawl out/ the worms play pinochle on

Your snout/ they eat your eyes, they eat your nose/they eat the jelly between your toes. A great big worm with rolling eyes/ Crawls in your stomach and out your eyes. Your stomach turns a slimy green/ and pus pours out like whipping cream. You spread it on a slice of bread/ and that's what worms eat when you're dead. The worms crawl in and the worms crawl out, and that's the end, so have no doubt."

I think my gramps would have liked to have us kids nearby to dance around his grave. He would have joined us with his fiddle and led the march himself at the cemetery, and had as much fun as we did. After a while, though, I didn't come as often and I missed him terribly, but the rains had begun, and coming up the hill slip sliding all the way, didn't make much sense anymore.

It was after my beloved Grandfather had died that my great aunt Pearl surrounded me with her tender love. She tried to help me though the sadness I felt about his passing. I felt so close to her at that time. Pearl was a docile and sweet tempered child, or so I heard from Great Grandma Willamina. She had been timid and shy, as different as night and day from her older sister. As a younger woman, while Maude was gone, and married to Bobbie Joe, Pearl had fallen in love. Her beau had been a logger named Jim McCoy, who drove a truck and hauled the lumber down to the docks to be shipped out by water to the Redwood Lumber Company down in Pittsburg. Pearl and Jim had run away to get married and to escape the family and Guerneville. The young couple bought a house down in Antioch. Her husband got a job at the Redwood Manufacturing plant and all was going well for them until her husband was killed. They had been married only six months. It was such a sad story, that I began to cry over the heartbreak that poor Pearl had to endure.

After her husband's death, Pearl visited her parents and by that time Maude again was in control of everything. Pearl was told to rent her house in Antioch and come back home. She got a job at the Guerneville Grocers and sent as much of her check as she could to pay on the mortgage, hoping to return one day to live in her own home. She was also made to sign a statement to the effect that she would stay and take care of her parents for the rest of their lives in exchange for the Guerneville homestead.

Within a couple of years my great grandparents, the Faylors were buried in the Guerneville Cemetery in the plot next to the Simpsons. Willamina died of pneumonia and Orson followed her two years later. During this time, my mother came back home. She had heard of the passing of her parents and both she and my Aunt Claudia showed up. Maude never said a word, but went about the business of getting through the burial and mourning period. My mother and aunt Claudia moved in with my Great Grandma, Grandpa and my great aunt Pearl in the small house next to us. Pearl had worked for years in the small grocery store in Guerneville from ten in the morning until six o'clock, and always ate dinner with us, but it seemed strange now to have my mother and aunt Claudia with us now. My mother's return meant nothing to me. She was a stranger who had appeared on our doorstep without warning. The ripples of her coming barely registered in the whirlpool of my mind. My thoughts were on the coming move away from what I had always known.

It was the end of my childhood of living with Maude and Bobbie Joe in this most wonderful of small mountain towns where I could swim in its rivers and roams its hills; a place where I could allow my imagination to drift and dream impossible dreams as I lay in the grass up in those hills and stare at the sky blue pink clouds rolling by.

Chapter 6

When it was all over, two months after both of my great grandparent's death, a moving van came up to our house and we began packing and carrying everything we had out to the yard where it was placed into a van. We said good-by to our friends and neighbors and we moved to Pearl's house in East Contra Costa County where she and her husband Jim McCoy had lived at 521 19th Street. My mother, Rosemary, had married for the third time and we all moved together into the main house. It was much too crowded for all of us to sleep there. At first we slept in a tent in the back yard. In a few weeks Earl, Mom's new husband, went to San Francisco where the city was selling off these large Municipal streetcars for the paltry sum of two hundred dollars. It was delivered by freight train and moved into the back of the main house. Earl and some buddy of his who did carpentry on the side, created a quaint living quarters that my mother, her new husband and we girls would occupy. My grandmother, Maude quickly found a new husband and she and my new grandfather, Fern, (now ain't that a strange moniker?) and aunt Pearl, lived in the main house. Maude now took over the mortgage, charging my mother and her husband ten dollars a month to rent the space on the land that the streetcar occupied.

A cement foundation had been laid and piers set in so that the original oak floors of the streetcar remained. Three steps led into a small kitchen with a specially built table set between the original leather seats, enough so that four people could dine at the same time. The space across was about twelve foot and allowed enough room for the cooking, sleeping and eating areas. The train windows were kept intact and provided plenty of light. A small hall led into the living room, and beyond were two bedrooms with the hall running along the original structure. A regular wallboard was used to divide the rooms.

My new grandfather, Fern Simmons, quickly took the place of Bobbie Joe. He was quick-witted, funny, and loved us as much as my old gramps. Maude continued to rule over her new kingdom. Claudia had moved on, taking Evelyn, Joe and Clifford with her. It seemed strange at first. My cousins had lived with us all of their live and now we had gone our separate ways. It would be many years after we moved that I would see them again. We would not leave Guerneville forever though, but continued to travel in a brand new black Buick as we had in the past. We loaded the car with picnic baskets and lots of "coke", my grandmother, Maude's, favorite beverage. She drank a dozen bottles a day, as she had in the past. It was not until I reached adulthood that I recognized her addition. It was why she was so mellow when we had our picnics at the beach in Bodega Bay and Armstrong Park

The town of Antioch was very different from its next-door neighbors of Pittsburg. Neither compared favorably to our Guerneville home. Located near the Sacramento—San Joaquin Rivers, this delta town was settled by a religious leader, William Wiggins Smith and his brother, Joseph. They were preachers from Maine who first settled in Pittsburg, then moved to Antioch, a town that would be known for the factories located near the river. The offensive smell of the Fiberboard manufacturing company, producing every kind of paper product imaginable, and the Crown Zellerback Company were both located on Wilber Avenue, very close to the Sacramento and San Joaquin Rivers. They employed many of the residents of Antioch. The Western California Cannery located on the other side of town competed with the canneries in Pittsburg, and hiring many of the Italians who lived there. The cannery also competed or rather mingled with the smell of the Fiberboard. The odor of tomatoes, prepared for canning, emitted a sickening sweet smell, permeating the atmosphere already polluted with factories and our olfactory receptors playing around our sensory conductors were on overload. A drive-in theater was built just a few blocks from the factories on Wilber Avenue. I suppose the citizens of Antioch had become somewhat immune to the smells, but I never did, and in my memories of my childhood when I speak of that time, I can recall all of it.

It was a small town, close-knit if you were a long time resident, but his grave. He would have joined us with his fiddle and led the march himself at the cemetery, and had almost as much fun as we did.

Marti Aiello

After a while, though, I didn't come so often, and coming up the hill slip sliding all the way, didn't make much sense anymore.

Grandpa Fern worked at the office of Columbia Steel Company in Antioch and my stepfather, Earl, worked in the open-hearth. They worked different shifts and slept while we were awake. He came home from the mill looking like a raccoon. Dirt and sweat streaked his face badly in need of a bath before he could join us for a meal, mostly the produce from our garden and hen house.

Maude had managed to find enough left over space between our living quarters to plant tomatoes, potatoes, carrots and squash, providing the major part of our cooking supplies. My grandpa, Fern, had built a hen house in the very first years we came to live here. Things had not changed much. Grammy still worked us in the garden and doing chores around the house whenever she spotted us sitting down for a little rest after school. It was 1940, and the neighborhood had its backyard gardens and fruit trees, like every other small town in America.

Rosie and I started school and life went on, not like it was living with my grandmother, Maude, but somewhat the same when it came to who was in charge. We lived within a stone's throw from the school. I was now in my first year at Antioch High School. Rosie was in Junior high, located behind the high school. It was very different from our years in Guerneville. Everything was new to us, and making friends was a bit difficult. The children of the long-time residents owned the right to form clicks. Newcomers were ignored, shunned or designated to second-class groups that formed around the natural leaders. The streets were alive with children going to and from school. My mother and Earl both worked. Mom was working in a cleaning shop in Pittsburg, and occasionally brought home clothes that had been left in the shop for over six months. When they weren't working, Mom and Earl spent time in Blu's Bar, drinking and having a good time. The town of Pittsburg, just five miles west of here, was where we went shopping for our school clothes in the J. C. Penny store or the Gay Shop on Railroad Avenue.

The downtown was the biggest I had ever seen. All sorts of shops were located on the main street and down the side streets, clear down to the river. The wartime economy brought soldiers from Camp Stoneman, and sailors from Port Chicago to visit the little town of Antioch. The USO was packed with military men that had come home on leave and those visiting from the camps. The old downtown of Pittsburg was heavily policed, cops kept an eye on the drunks that created the usual number of bar brawls. Because of the large military base located at Camp Stoneman in Pittsburg, taxis ran constantly between the camp and the downtown area. Saloons were the first to occupy an expanding business district. Jewelry stores, pharmacies and a number of new clothing stores also opened to accommodate the new population of military personnel.

I went to my first football game in my whole life. Our team called the "Panthers" were playing against the Pittsburg Pirates. The rivalry was more that just between the football teams The two small towns of Pittsburg and Antiocoh had been in competition with one another since the first businessman, Reverend, W. W. Smith first opened a two-story hotel and dining room near the waterfront in Pittsburg and later moved five miles east and named the settlement, Antioch.

Most of the people living in the town of Pittsburg were Italians. The Antioch boys used to mix it up with Pittsburg boys; I mean bloody noses and broken bones kind of fights. It was at one of the Friday night games that I met John. He was cute, a little older than me. I was fourteen and he was nineteen and we fell in love. I have to confess that John went a little further than Daryl Dudley Holymeyr. It was my first summer in Antioch after we left Guerneville and between the boys at school and the boys from the Camp, I was having a grand time.

Every Saturday night me and Rosie would sneak out and go riding with a bunch of rough boys from school. I had borrowed my mother's good pedal pushers and a tight sweater. A fellow named "Angel" borrowed his father's Cadillac convertible. About eight kids piled aboard and we rode around the country road towards Oakley. On this occasion, the boys demanded that we "put out or get out" of the car.

Me and Rosie and a girl named Joan were left stranded along the highway. We walked, and then walked some more back to the outskirts of Pittsburg and Antioch where we stopped at my friend Joan's house and called my mother to pick us up. I was more afraid of my mother finding out about her pants than I was about the inconvenience of making a trip to pick us up.

37

All of us, my sister and I, and my mother quietly entered our house, careful not to wake Grammy and face the fury that she was able to inflict on her recalcitrant children and grandchildren. Maude was still in charge and would be until her dying day. Everything we did was watched and monitored by my grandmother. But we all became adept at quiet and willful disobedience. It seemed to give us more pleasure and a sharp edged, but false sense of control.

Chapter 7

Shortly after we moved to Antioch, Fern bought a nice black Buick for Maude. It was her birthday. We took long rides on Sundays, traveling the roads of highway 4 all the way along the river route to Sacramento. Maude became enchanted with San Francisco. She and Fern spent nearly every weekend touring around China Town, and later Maude went alone. She picked up souvenirs at first, then more exotic items. Within a short time, she hired some carpenters to build a second floor onto the house; a structure that looked like the top of a pagoda. It was eight-sided and every other one was topped with little wings that slanted upwards. It looked to be about ten foot high. One could enter by way of a curving stairway that was just about three foot wide. It took three months to complete. When the quality of work did not suit her, she could be heard from a block away. "You knuckleheads are gonna have to take that down and start doing what I tell you to do.

Don't you have any brains at all? Now git busy and rip that out and do it right." The concept that somehow had logged itself into Maude's imaginative brain was not translated properly to the bewildered carpenters, and many of the workmen had quit after a couple of weeks. She would hire a couple more and little by little, progress was made. I am quite sure that the local carpenters had never encountered a request to build a structure like this, or work for a woman who demanded as much from them.

For three months, from our house in the Streetcar, we heard Grammy shouting at the workmen. Peace and calm was not restored until the last nail was driven into the little pagoda and the last drop of red paint embellished the little wings pointing toward the sky. At last when the building was completed, she locked the beautifully carved door and no one could enter except my Grandmother. It was her sanctuary, she declared. The top floor was completely hidden from the outside by the full-grown fig trees in our yard.

As I look back on those years, I wondered about Grandpa Fern. How strange it seems now that he was so uninvolved in the things that my Grandmother did. Had she taken control of him as she had with all of us? The poor man had somehow fallen under the spell of Maude and never recovered his wits was my perception. Even at my age, just fourteen years old, I had learned that you needed to have a thick skin, and give her wide birth, and stay out of arms reach.

A USO club was operating in the old VFW building and I went with a girlfriend every Saturday night. It was there that I met Bob Davidson, my first husband, and he had asked me to marry him. He was in the Navy at Port Chicago. Grammy attempted to impart a bit of Sex Education by saying "Get it over with, go up and down and in and out . . . That's the way it works." But when I found out I was pregnant my grandmother had a fit. As a consequence, my mother and her husband, Earl, summarily escorted us to Reno. And after a ten-minute ceremony, we went to our rented rooms at Motel 6. When I had undressed, I got into bed and pulled up the covers up to my chin and struck my nose in the process, causing it to bleed profusely. The honeymoon plans were aborted, and my mother was called to get an ice pack and the hotel maid called to change the bloody sheets. This event portended a murky future, I thought. This was my first brush with matrimony, well perhaps a bit more than a brush, more like the time it takes to beget five children, total. But, that's another story.

After I had married Bob, he was doing duty in San Diego, so I continued to date John. He was my first love. I fell for him when I was fourteen years old. We were so close it hurt to leave him. Bob was always at sea, I felt like I really didn't get a chance to know my husband, he was gone so much, what could I do? John and I dated openly, going to school dances and the movies. The local theater featured live entertainment, with San Francisco celebrities like Carol Doda, a beautiful strip-teaser who showed her 'wares' in this once proper home of dignified families with Methodist leanings, and church-going, simple folk. The strangest thing happened during this time. The El Campanile Theater had special entertainment on the weekends, and John and I went to a show featuring Sally Rand, the famous San Francisco fan dancer who stripped down to the least amount of covering permissible under the law. She and the girls in the chorus line had these large peacock feathers that were used to cover those parts unmentionable. I couldn't believe my eyes when I looked up and saw the well-known star was really my grandfather's Sally. I could never forget those eyes, those lips and that way she had of entering a room and enhancing the very presence of wherever she found herself. I felt like I was ten years old again and I wanted to grow up and be just like Sally. I turned to John who sat transfixed by what was happening on stage. "John, I know Sally Rand." I said.

John raised his eyebrows. You know Sally Rand?"

"Yes, I do."

"How could you know Sally Rand?"

"She was my grandfather's girl friend."

"Oh yeah?" he said, like I was lying.

"I'll prove it to you. After the show is over, we can go down to the dressing room and talk to her."

"Okay, sure." Still not convinced that I knew her. 'Well, I'll show him,' I thought.

The show went on and the audience screamed, applauded and made 'cat calls' ten minutes after the curtain went down. We waited until the majority of the people had gone out before we attempted to get by the ushers and make our way down stairs. We didn't know where we were going until I saw a star on the door of one of the rooms. We knocked then knocked a second time.

"Who is it?" a woman's voice called out.

"It's me, Lynette Simpson, Sally. My grandfather was Bobbie Joe Simpson.

"Lynette Simpson? Just a minute honey, let me get some clothes on."

"I'll wait. I have my boyfriend with me Sally. Is that okay?"

"Sure kid. Be right with you."

She came out of the dressing room and opened the door. "Come on in Honey." She looked at John. "Hello, big boy." She said, moving her head to the side and looking up at John with those enormous blue eyes. They were especially large, with a dark ring around the lids, arched eyebrows and enough paint and face powder to cover the obvious wrinkles that make-up couldn't conceal. "So this is your boyfriend, Lynette? You sure can pick 'em, Honey."

"It sure is nice to see you Sally." I couldn't believe it. But I knew when you walked out on the stage, the way you looked, I just knew it was you. Did you come to my grandfather's funeral Sally?

"Yeah, that was me Lynette, I couldn't talk to you of course, because you were with all of your family, and I didn't want to start a war with your grandmother."

"I'm glad you came, Sally."

"Lynette, some time when you're a little older, I want you to come and see me in San Francisco."

"Gee, Sally, thanks, I'd like that too." She looked at me and then handed me her calling card. I looked at John and then we said our 'goodbye's and left. The card was printed with her name in fancy scroll and her telephone number in the corner.

"Are you going to get in touch with her sometime?" John asked.

"I don't know, maybe." After that John dropped me off at my house, and I snuck around the back of our streetcar house and tapped the window to get Rosie's attention so she could help me in. Mom and Earl were probably out at the bars, but I couldn't take the chance with Grammy next door probably looking out of her window. She had caught me out late once before, and woke up the neighborhood with her yelling.

It was about this time that my father tracked us down and came to see me in Antioch. My grandmother saw him and threatened to bash him over the head with an iron frying pan. He stood out in the back yard, yelling. "Lynette and Rosie are my kids, and I have every right to see them."

"You git your skinny ass off my property or I'm calling the police."

"I'm not leaving until I can talk to my kids, you old bat."

Grammy called the police and they escorted my father out of town. It was the first and last time I saw him. It was years later that I found out about another grandmother I had and went to visit her in Richmond. She was an old woman at that time. She cried when I introduced myself. We visited for an afternoon as she told me about her son, my father, who was too young when he married my mother and regretted his neglect and absence from his family and his duty to us. I listened in silence as she rambled on. It meant nothing to me. I never knew a father and never would. Grammy was mother, father and grandparent, all wrapped up in one package. The rest of them were absent non-entities who lacked rights to me, and there was nothing they could give me to make up for what they lost.

Chapter 8

It wasn't too long after I began to 'show' that I had to quit school. Bob was still in the service and came home some weekends from Mare Island. I moved into a small apartment in Vallejo, and lived with the very basic necessities. It was a cold-water flat, no washrooms and I had to wash the clothes and sheets out in a small sink, wringing them dry by hand and hanging them on a wooden rack. I moved back home to Antioch. My mother had divorced Earl and moved on. I never saw her again. And Bob shipped out to the warfront in the pacific. My baby boy, Jimmy, was born in May of 1942. After the war, my husband, Bob Davison, divorced me and went back to his hometown in Chickasaw, Alabama, where he was reunited with his childhood sweetheart. That was husband number one.

Number two was a fellow named Jimmy Lappstick. Our marriage lasted four years. We had three children together in that time. James Junior, Lilly and a boy named Kenny who had succumbed to pneumonia at two years of age. Jimmy was probably one of the laziest men I had ever met. He was gone from home more than he was present. He spent his days at the bars and his nights playing black Jack and poker. The times he spent at home was usually spent in bed. I was working in Brentwood and Byron at the time, picking tomatoes from the farms and fruit and nuts from the orchards. After a few years, I knew that this marriage was not going to last. One night I had met up with Jim at a saloon in downtown Pittsburg as he sat on a stool at the bar, a pretty young girl draped over his shoulders as he caressed his glass of beer. I went up to the bar, sat next to them and ordered a shot of whiskey, which I poured over his head. He turned around with a drunken look on his face and said he wanted a divorce. I laughed and exited, stage right.

Number three was Darrel Scott. He was also a Navy man who had lived on the base in Port Chicago. His military experience had created a monster. His expectation was such that he demanded strict obedience from the children and his wife. Punishment was meted out in response to any undisciplined behavior. When I came from work, my kids were usually sitting quietly anticipating his moves as he dominated us all with his presence. The light-hearted laughter that we enjoyed before our marriage was gone. In its place was a hard-hearted man who took delight in having the power to control our very lives. I wanted this marriage to work. I needed a father for my children and a safe haven to come home to. I got neither. My oldest boy, Jim, had a number of "accidents" and I began to suspect that my husband caused them. Jimmy had suffered a broken arm and was now in a sling. He did not speak of how it happened, he simply looked to Darrel to tell me the story and when he didn't, Jimmy just lowered his eyes as the tears rolled down his cheeks.

"Did you hurt my son?" I asked.

"You've done such a lousy job as a mother, I had to teach him a few lessons."

"Get out of this house you son of a bitch. Right now." I added.

Darrell left and I knelt beside my boy and wept. We both did. Lilly, who had a frightened look on her face as she listened to the shouting, joined us. I sat there on the floor, surrounded by my babies, until they fell asleep in my arms.

I had a job, but I couldn't handle the expense of a sitter, so I brought the children over to my grandmother. She was getting older, but still she could handle them until I could back on my feet. I couldn't afford to keep the apartment and so I stayed with friends here and there until I could found a way out of debt again. I had bought furniture and appliances on time when Darrell and I had married, now I couldn't pay for them. I was out of a job, out of money and out on the streets. It was wintertime and I could not work in the fields, orchards or canneries. Finally, I did get a job cleaning the bars and clubs that we had frequented. It was then I was hired to work with the bartender when needed and to act as stage manager, introducing the audiences to the topless dancers that the owner had hired to attract more customers.

The small towns east of Antioch were: Oakley, Brentwood and Byron. The common link with these communities, were the farms

45

spread beyond the cluster of homes and businesses in town. Fields of spinach, tomatoes and corn were interspersed with acres of peaches and apricot trees and vineyards. Walnut and almond trees spread leafy limbs in long even rows, running east to Byron and west to Antioch. Many of the transit people who worked seasonally stayed in small shacks on the farm property, cooking and eating in tents spread out like the carnival grounds. Shelters were erected and full of families who followed the picking seasons during the early spring until late September.

It was in Byron that I got a job picking tomatoes, my back bent over the long rows, pulling the fruit off the vine and tossing the ones to be used for canning onto a harvester. Later after I had worked in the tomato patches a few weeks, I became part of one group of ladies who stood on the side of the harvester, pulling ripe tomatoes off a belt that went round and round, discarding the rotten or soft tomatoes. The two belts ran in different directions with another group of women on the other side. What was really hilarious was the group on one side were Christian ladies singing church hymns and on the other side of the harvester were the others singing a raucous chorus of 'Roll me Over," much louder, and in far less harmony. I don't suppose it would not be too difficult to guess where I stood.

Another job was cleaning the many bars that lined the streets of historic downtown Antioch. I quickly moved up to become a supervisor in charge of, and announcing, the topless dancers who performed in a bar called "The Living End." It was located just outside the town, and frequented by the hard drinkers who sat at the bars, nursing a beer with an occasional shot of whiskey by a likeable bartender as he moved up and down chatting with good humor with the "regulars". When the dancers entered from the back room. Heads swiveled around, back to the bar, as I made my entrances and introduced my "girls". Most were between thirty and forty years old. Sagging breasts were uplifted, and roughed cheeks, eyes ringed with back pencil and bleached blond hair tended to make them appears as look-alikes. They danced, bumping and grinding to the snare drums of the three—piece band playing music.

Moving up the ladder, I landed a job working a Canteen truck, delivering food for constructions sites. One unenviable day during a particular heavy rainfall, dressed in my white uniform and shoes, I delivered food to the workmen who were setting up a new housing track. I stopped the truck short of the muddy plots of land and was urged on by the workers. "Come a little closer, Lynette, you can't leave until I get my men fed," said the foreman.

"I don't think I can come in, I might get stuck."

"We'll take care of you, Lynette, now get the truck over here." They shouted. So I gunned the truck and half way over the wheels spun round and round. I wasn't going anywhere. I got down from the truck, opened the side of the canteen, filled the calls for orders of sandwiches, salads and cupcakes, and plunged toward the waiting customers. My white shoes were covered, sucking up the mud in noisy 'plops' as I carried the food back and forth until all were fed. The truck was thoroughly stuck and one of the workmen brought in a Caterpillar and hauled the truck back to the main road. I took the truck back, washed it and myself clean, turned in my 'take', got my final pay and resigned.

The third match made of need to find a father for my two children, was Jerry Sears. At the time, I had been going with a married man named Barney and besides the "visits" and the steady dates, drinking and dancing at various bars, my life took on a lighthearted tone. My need for companionship and a little fun in my life was fully supplied. Barney's wife perhaps knew and endured, or was complicit in allowing him the freedom he needed in exchange for room and board and the sanctity of marriage, being catholic and all, it seemed to work for a long time. Eighteen years in fact. Barney treated her so badly that his wife finally left him, taking everything. He moved me into his house and I became his for good. I, however, wanted more and when Jerry Sears came into my life and offered marriage, I accepted. It wasn't the end of Barney, though. When Jerry and I were out for the evening with mutual friends, Barney had not given up the key to my house and would sometimes be found naked in my bed when we returned home. He pulled all kinds of shenanigans like wrecking Jerry's car and finally, Jerry filed for divorce. I felt like a puppet on a string. I couldn't figure myself out. I really did not have an identity of my own, but assumed the persona of whatever was required of me. As the years went by Barney's wife finally left him and they were divorced. We married and I had my last child with him. It was a girl we named Jeanie and she adored her father, and he spoiled her, it was my fourth marriage and my last. When he became a father, I became his servant. One day he ordered me to

"Go to your room, Lynette." My anger got the best of me. I picked up the pot of spaghetti that I had just made and threw it across the room and ran away from home. I drove to Tahoe. I called later and Barney gave me permission to come home. When I did, he asked me to get down on my knees and apologize to everyone. It was little wonder that my kids had the same attitude toward me. No respect was given, and I guess no respect was expected.

Barney was about ten years older than I, and when we had been married a short time he had a heart attack and I needed to find work again. At that time while Barney did nothing but sit in a chair demanding service, I began operating a home-catering service for a few years until a better job offer came through the R.O.P. office. I had received training and a G.E.D. certificate, plus a two-year stint at Junior College. My need for a real job eventually drove me into law enforcement. I became a Sheriff's Assistant after previously working in jobs less than appealing, and working harder for far less money. It was time to move on. That was when I was hired by the county and worked myself up to the Sheriff's Assistant job. The only caveat was that those hired wore no 'big' hair, 'no boobs hanging out or lateness. I donned a khaki uniform, black dress shoes and black belt. I must say I looked pretty spiffy. I think I may have been thirty-five at that time. The passing of years brought me no closer to happiness than the earlier years. Barney had given up on life and became a self-proclaimed invalid. His arteries were clogged with cholesterol because of the amount of 'junk' food he ate. By that time we had been married and together for many years, he died one day as he sat in the rocker in the living room. I had discovered his cold body when I returned from work on the 3-11 shift. I felt no remorse . . . happy to be free of the obligations I had felt in caring for him.

After his death, things were going fairly well. I worked at my job, the pay was good and all of my kids were in school.

It was during this time that I received a frantic call from a neighbor living next door to Maude. "Get over here Lynette, the streetcar's on fire. I called the fire department and they are just getting their hoses out. Come quick."

I was getting ready to go on the night shift. I would have been gone had I received the call five minutes earlier. I jumped into my truck and broke speed records in my haste get to the house. My grandmother was just emerging from her front door asking, "What's going on here and why are those men here?"

"Where's Pearl, grammy?

"How in the hell should I know?" She replied.

I hailed one of the firemen and told him that my Aunt Pearl might be in the fire.

"Call for an ambulance, Bob." He yelled at one of the firemen. "Let's go men, someone may still be in the house." He shouted.

The fire hoses were shooting out water as a couple of men ran toward the door calling her name. "The bedrooms are toward the end of the house." I shouted.

The first man to emerge from the still burning, now smoke-filled building was carrying the still form of my Aunt Pearl. "Is she alive?" I asked. He shook his head but didn't answer me.

"Get the ambulance crew over here and take this lady into the hospital—hurry!" he shouted.

It was weeks before my aunt Pearl was able to leave the hospital. She had suffered smoke inhalation and was burned on her right side. The fireman had brought a wet blanket and had immediately wrapped her in it . . . saving her life, and when the burns were healed, she had little disability.

The police were called in and the cause of the fire was determined to be a deliberate act of arson. The streetcar had been totally destroyed by the fire, and everything in it was gone. After talking with Maude, who was the only one home at the time, and Fern who had been at a V.F.W. meeting, they never found the culprit who had started the fire. I had my suspicions, and when all was done and Pearl released from the hospital, I took her home to live with me. She gladly watched the children, and I paid her the wages that I would have paid a sitter. Just as we had all of the years that we lived with my grandmother and grandfathers, we played games during the evenings at home before bedtime for the kids, and my shift work schedule. Aunt Pearl was good at pinochle, monopoly or other board games and she rarely lost, except to 'fudge' a little to allow the little ones a victory now and then. These were some of the best years of my life. Aunt Pearl cooked and kept the house tidy. The kids were still small and did not cause me too much grief except for the usual trips to the hospital for stitches or assorted illnesses and injuries. I had sworn off men for the time being. No more pregnancies, no more nagging and no more than the usual ups and downs of life.

Chapter 9

I now had the leisure time to relax after breakfast or lunch and read a book now and then. I had collected many novels throughout the years and would never have the opportunity to finish them. On one momentous day, a rainy, cold day in March, I had picked up a book and turned to a marker, the card that Sally Rand had given me many years ago. I had entirely forgotten about my grandfather, Bobbie Joe's old flame. The card was discolored, dogged and earmarked but still readable. 'Miss Sally Rand', was written in eloquent, sweeping letters across the card, with a faded telephone number on the back. I sat down in the chair next to the telephone stand and dialed the number, not knowing whether she may have changed it over the twenty years since I had seen her at the El Campanile Theater. A woman with a southern accent, probably a maid, had answered the call.

"Is this the residence of Miss Sally Rand?" I inquired.

"Yes, Mum, it is."

"Is Miss Rand in?

"No Mum, but if you would like to leave a message and a number, I'll tell her you called."

"Thank you." I replied.

In less than two hours, Sally called me back.

"Lynette?"

"It's me Sally, I found your telephone number and decided to call. Do you think we might be able to meet somewhere? It would be nice to see you again, that is if you're not too busy."

"Yes. I really didn't know where you lived or how to get in touch with you, but I'm glad you called honey. Would you like to get together?"

"Hey, that would be swell."

"I live in Belmont, give me your address and I'll send the address and the directions to my place. Just tell me when you want to come and I'll have a nice lunch or dinner waiting."

"That would be great, Sally. Goodbye now." I hung up and sat in the chair and felt special that she had asked me to come to her house. She must have a mansion, I thought, with the money she made as an entertainer, and I heard she was one of the big-time 'Madam's' of all time. I couldn't wait to hear from her again. When she called again the following week, we set a date for Sunday. I hadn't told anyone about Sally Rand, not even Aunt Pearl, I promised my grandfather and I had kept my promise all these years. I went over to Macy's in Concord and bought a new suit for the occasion. I was a little nervous about the visit. It seemed so strange to get together with a real celebrity. When Sunday rolled around, I told Aunt Pearl that I needed to go and visit a friend over in the City. Following the directions that Sally gave me, I arrived at her home at one O'clock. When I saw the address on the iron-gated estate, I was overwhelmed. A man in uniform opened the gate and called the house for instructions. I was impressed. She was at the door just seconds after I had rung the bell.

"Lynette?"

I shook my head. "Yes, it's me Sally. I guess I changed some since you saw me last."

"Honey, you're as pretty as you were when you were just a teen-ager. Come on in. I've got someone here I want you to meet."

I looked at her curiously, not knowing what to think. An older man had been sitting in a dark green velvet chair in this large sitting room. He came toward me with his arms outstretched.

"Lynette. Don't you remember me?"

His hair was almost white, and his posture a little stooped. There was something about him that I found familiar. It was his eyes, still blue, crinkled at the sides. It was my grandfather, Bobbie Joe, in the flesh. My jaw dropped open. Tears began rolling down my face. I felt confused, angry and relieved that he was alive.

"How could you do that? You walked away and I felt abandoned. Don't you know how afraid I was? You were the only solid thing in my life, and then you were gone." "You're not dead at all."

"Not yet honey. Come on it and sit down and I'll tell you all about my accident."

I walked toward the couch, my legs not quite steady. "I don't understand. I saw the picture of you, falling through the air. You couldn't have survived a fall like that Grandpa."

"It wasn't me, Lynette. It was a guy, must have been a street bum, who had fallen from a rooftop on a job I was working. Sally and some fellows we knew were waiting for me to finish a job. They brought up a plan to free me from your grandmother, Maude. If I had tried to divorce her, she would have killed me. No doubt about it. So this was an opportunity to get out without all the rigmarole of dealing with trying to get away from a rotten marriage. So the plan was for me to change clothes with this dead guy who was so mangled you couldn't tell who he was, and disappear."

"But what about the picture? I still have it at home."

"Well, that was also part of the plan. We took the fellow that had been killed back up to the roof and the guy that was in on the plot took the picture as the man was falling a second time. He stayed on the scene long enough to talk with the cops that had been called about the accident, and he showed them his camera and told this whopper about how he captured the picture as the man was falling from this big rigging I was working on."

I just stared at my grandfather and Sally for a minute, and I began to laugh hysterically. I couldn't stop. The two of them looked at me curiously, and then joined in the laughter. We must have laughed for ten minutes. It was ludicrous. One of us would stop and then look at the other and start again. I know it was part of releasing the tension

53

that all of us must have felt; them in telling the story, me in listening to the crazy, wild tale of a man trying to escape the tyranny of an impossible marriage to an impossible woman.

"I can only ask you Lynette, that you don't tell your grandma."

"I never told anyone our secrets Grandpa, not ever. I'm just glad you're not dead and that you are living a happy life."

"Well, now that's over, lets sit down and have our meal." Sally rung a bell, and a servant came in. "Please bring the food, Fredrick, and open a nice bottle of wine. Thank you."

The man disappeared and some women dressed in white, brought in several courses of the best food I ever experienced. This would be the first of many visits to my Grandpa Bobbie Joe and Sally Rand. We grew closer as the years went by.

After the shock of seeing my grandfather Bobbie Joe alive, my life went on as usual. One day following another, the kids fussing and fuming over minor incidents. Jeanie was a moody kid growing up. She would disappear for hours into her room, sometimes reading racy magazines or novels, sometimes covering her head with a lacy black covering and attending Catholic services every morning for months and then suddenly abandoning the church all together. One of the most lasting, hilarious events was the time Jeanie had found religion after two nice looking boys on bicycles had stopped by the house. Following an hour spent talking with the two young men, I had called Jeanie in for dinner. At first she sat down in her usual place, then rose and declared. "I really don't care to eat with you Catholics." I almost choked on my food, as she stalked out of the room with her dinner plate in hand, and she ate all her meals in her room for the next two months.

As long as Fern lived, Grammy required weekly visits from me now and wouldn't come to my house as long as Aunt Pearl lived there. I hoped my aunt would live forever. Grammy called to tell us that Grandpa Fern had suffered a heart attack. He was gone within two weeks following a stroke. Again, we buried another family member, but this time at the local Holy Rosary Cemetery in Antioch. This long-suffering, patient old man was finally at rest. Just a few months later, I began to notice the changes in Maude. With no one to dictate to, no one to play cards or board games with, she began to make friends with the neighbors. This would not seem strange in any other person with a normal desire to reach out to others, but it was exceedingly strange for Maude.

Numerous cats had made themselves welcome in the once tidy house. The stink was prevalent as I stood outside of the torn screen door. The door handle and knob was thick with a sticky substance and I was loathed the touch it. With no one to respond to an order for her list of work to be done in the house or garden, she neglected herself and her home. When I would visit for a time, dishes were laid throughout the house and kittens that had not been trained used every corner. Eventually, Maude would not let me in the house. I brought her groceries and paid her bills, but that's all she allowed me to do.

There were some good years and some bad. Filling the needs of four rebellious teenagers and the ever-increasing demands of a capricious grandmother took its toll on my frayed nerves. While at work on Sunday night, the night clerk was absent and I filled in for her. During the processing of an angry drunken sot, I received a call from a Lieutenant Andrews that my daughter, Lilly, had wrecked my car and was held at the Pittsburg police station on drunk driving charges. We were short-handed, more than the usual problem drunks and angry felons had crossed my path that night and I couldn't leave my job. I called a friend to bail Lilly out and told her I would be home at the end of my shift. When Monday morning dawned, Sheriff Brown came in to relieve me.

"What's going on Lynette? Where's the intake report? How in the hell can I run a department when the staff can't get her act together?" He stood there with his hands on his hips and stared at me. My usually friendly boss must have had a bad weekend, but he couldn't have had the year that I had experienced. My youngest daughter had run away four times in one year, we had to move three times in an eight-month's period of time, Jimmy had an appendectomy with serious complications. He almost died during the operation and developed a staff infection during his hospitalization. I began to cry.

"Look, Lynette, stop acting like a wussy woman and tell me what happened?"

I couldn't stop, I cried and then cried some more. Brown clumsily patted me on the shoulder and tried to calm me down. He called on one of the female staff to come over to our department. My friend, Lois, came in and took me in her arms. I continued to cry. Finally, they sent me over to the Martinez hospital, still crying. I couldn't seem to stop. Before it was all over, I had seen a regular doctor and three psychiatrists, and then I was released and given a month's leave to recuperate. Apparently, nothing was seriously wrong with me except the years of stress and anxiety had found its peak level and I broke under the duress of my grandmother's constant demands. Not just the on-going grueling demands of my teenaged children, but what had built up in my psyche over the years. It was not long after that episode in my life that the children had become much more concerned with pleasing me and taking care not to allow our usual conflicts to become out of control. After my hospitalization, our household became more peaceful. It was a good thing that had happened after all. But, as with all good things, it doesn't last forever.

I began to hear my grandmother talk about a woman who had befriended her as she became more unstable and unable to care for herself. The woman, Helene Borders, was with Maude every first of the month to take her to the bank where she cashed her check. Helene directed Maude to withdraw the money, about eight thousand dollars, and to put it into another account with Helene as co-signer. It would simplify things, she said. When I discovered the transfer, I had to get an attorney to get the money back into another account and assign myself, as next of kin, as executor. When the police were notified, the woman promptly disappeared and was never found. Unfortunately, I was now "on call" twenty-four hours a day. On my day off from night shift, I spent all the time cleaning out the filthy house that had been left in the hands of day caretakers. It took weeks before the house was put in some kind of order. I received calls in the middle of the night demanding that I get over to the house to take care of some problem or another.

One particular night, I went to my grandmother's house to discover her naked and covered with thousands of dollars of musty-smelling dirty money. "Where did you get this money?" I asked her. Her eyes were glowing like she was about to tell me the best kind of secret as she wagged her finger at me. She got up from the bed, her bony, wrinkled body covered with the dust of the 'filthy lucre', which was no longer a term used in the usual sense, but really filthy lucre. She looked insane as she cackled like the 'Wicked Witch of the West', her cheeks wrinkling in a hundred creases and her thin white hair standing up on her skull.

"There's more."

"You mean more money?"

"Of course I do, you idiot."

"Where did you hide it, Grammy?"

"Nobody can find it."

"I know, you are so smart, you hid it really well."

"And I'm not going to tell you."

"That's because you're lying."

With that she struck me across the mouth. It was sudden and painful, belying the fact of her strength, clothed in her fragile little body, but able to deliver a heavy punch. My lip was split and bleeding a little. She grabbed up as much money as she could carry while I was looking for a towel that I could wet to staunch the bleeding. With the money in her hands, mouth and every other crevice that would hold it, she ran naked out the front door and tripped over a stone in the garden, plunging into the rose bushes along side of the house. By the time I got out there to see what happened, she had dropped the bills and screamed with the pain in her hip. It was three o'clock in the morning when I placed a call to the hospital. "Could you send an ambulance to 529 19th Street, my grandmother fell and is in pain." I sat beside her, my one hand held the towel against my lip as I gathered the money she had dropped. I stuffed it in my pocket, then held my grandmother's head as she cried with the pain she was suffering.

When the ambulance came, they picked her up and took her away, I told them I would follow in my car in a few minutes. I went back into the house, took the keys out of my grandmother's purse, and locked up. After a few hours at the hospital, with Maude tucked securely in bed, I called Aunt Pearl. It was six o'clock. "Pearl, Grammy is in the hospital with a broken hip, I'll tell you more about that later. Just get the kids off to school and I'll probably be home around noon or so." I hung up and looked at myself in the mirror. My lower lip was swollen and discolored.

The cut was caking over with dried blood. I had told the emergency room nurse what had happened, and she conveyed it to the doctor. "My grandmother's house is in a deplorable condition, the stench is more that I can stand, could you give me a mask to wear so that I can go back and pick up some things for my grandmother?" I asked. "Of course," she said as handed me the mask. "Doctor Scott will perform the surgery on her this afternoon." I thanked her for her help and left. The time would allowed me a few hours, and days after that, to go back to the house and take care of the money that was scattered over the room and look for any more of Maude's hidden treasure.

It took hours to scour the house for money. Some had been hidden behind baseboards. I could tell where the casing had been pried open. Some was behind a tacked on board behind her clothes closet. It was like a treasure hunt and I forgot that I hadn't slept. A surge of energy and excitement with each new discovery kept me going for six straight hours. When I realized how much time had passed, I stopped to call my boss and told him about grandmother Maude's fall and subsequent hip surgery.

"Take as much time as you need, Lynette. I'll call in a replacement. Sorry about your grandmother."

"Thank you sir, I'll try to get back as soon as I can take care of some matters." I hung up the phone and thanked the gods that be for this wonderful day. My clothes were filthy with the handling of money and the search that pulled out as much dirt as money in Grammy's secret caches. "Oh my God!" I just remembered the top floor. The Pagoda that the carpenters had built for Maude the first years after we came to Antioch. My knees began to quiver, and my head was clouded with the vision of more money stacked in the pagoda, a whole room full. "Oh my God." I'll be a millionaire, I thought. I went to the narrow staircase that was built years ago. We had never been permitted to go near the steps. Now, I had access to the whole house. My heart was beating a hundred times a minute. I could feel my whole chest almost spastic. I had to sit down right where I was, in the dirty room on a dirty floor. After about twenty minutes, I got to my feet. I felt a little wobbly, but held my hand against the side of the walls and began to climb, slowly at first, then ten more steps to the door. I tried the knob. It wouldn't turn. "Damn it."

With my mouth full of silent curses, I hurried back down the stairs and into the kitchen to wash my face and hands. Taking a scrub brush that was in the laundry room, I swept it over my dirty uniform then locked the door to the house again and drove to the hospital. As I walked through the hall toward the nurse's station, passing by a mirrored brass plate, I saw the reflection of myself, head full of dust, unkempt hair in total disorder as I tried to untangle the mess that was me. The nurse that had taken care of my Grandmother was sitting at her chair as I approached the desk. "I need to take the things that Maude Simmons was wearing when she came into the hospital. Could you get them for me please?" I asked politely. "Of course, I have them in the locker room." She got up and disappeared down the hall. When she came back she was carrying a large plastic bag. "Here you are, check and see if everything is there." I did as she had instructed and found the string that Grammy always wore around her neck. The key was there! I breathed a sigh of relief, took the bag and left the hospital. As I headed toward 19th Street, the ride seemed to take forever before finally stepping into the house and running up the stairs again, this time with the key in hand.

My hand was on the knob, my heart throbbing against my chest again as I entered the room. What I saw was so unexpected, so unlike the room of a woman I had known all of my life. It was immaculate, almost devoid of furniture, the light from outside streamed in, creating a prism-like effect from the eight windows. A woven grass matt covered the floor, and a single black, lacquered table sat in the center of the room. In the middle of the table sat a hookah, a graceful tall glass container filled with clear fluid. A flexible tube about twelve inches long was wrapped once around the jar. My mind could not grasp what my eyes were seeing. I was a member of the Police Department, I knew what it looked like, this scene I observed before me, but my mind could not match up the evidence with my life and the life of Maude Simmons. I shook my head.

The vision did not disappear as I stared at the sight, not believing what I saw. My hands were grasping the sides of my head where a dull aching pain began to get my attention. I began to observe other things that were in this sparse room. Beautiful faded silk pillows were strewed around the room. The colors were blue, yellow and a shade of purple. I needed to get out of here, out of the room unlike any I could have envisioned. I backed out of this nightmare and tried to erase it from my mind. It didn't make any sense to me. Too much had happened for one twenty four hour period. Anything that I had experienced from my years at the Police Department was nothing compared to this last hour. I needed to regroup, to put this away for a while and concentrate on the reality of something I did understand . . . the money that I had found just hours ago. I'll think about this later when my head stops throbbing.

I didn't make it home by noon as I had promised Pearl, but she assured me that everything was under control and she would tend to the kids.

"Don't you worry Lynette, take as long as you need to, we'll be all right."

"Thanks Pearl, I'll be home this evening for sure. I'm trying to clean things up around the house. When I finish here I'll be back, but probably late." I hung up the phone and rested a little, finishing off some leftover chicken from the refrigerator. As I sat at the table, it occurred to me to push the refrigerator out, and lo and behold, I found paper sacks stuffed with twenty-dollar bills, and one with fifty-dollar bills. Would it never end? O happy day, I hope not yet! I began to sing, "Oh Happy Day, Oh Happy Day, when Jesus comes, when Jesus comes." Oh yeah!

I was tired and very dirty, and sniffed under my arms as I looked around for something to wear. Slipping a towel around my body I threw the dirty clothes into the washing machine. My energy was quickly fading as the excitement of the day wore off. So much had happened; Grammy's accident, the hospital, the found money, the discovery of my Grandmother's hidden vices, was all too much to think about. My head ached as I spread a blanket over a chair and sat down and waited for my clothes to dry.

Dressed now, I began to count and stack the bills into piles of twenties, fifties and hundreds. When I finished I had counted eighty thousand dollars total. The fives and tens, I stuck in my purse until it bulged. At ten o'clock PM, I put the whole amount into a grocery box labeled "Bananas" and put it in the back of my car. I drove home slowly, savoring the delicious feeling of freedom from my indentured service to my grandmother and the wonderful future of spending freely on the 'good things in life," O yeah! I began to feel very kindly toward old Maude. Maybe we had our differences, but heck, it wasn't all that bad. And having a windfall of eighty thousand dollars eased the pain a whole lot. And this is the best part. Nobody knew about it. "Holy Shit!" How am I ever going to explain this to the bank teller if I want to put it in a safe place and earn a little interest on it? I'll put it all in a safety deposit box until I work it all out.

When I got home, everyone was down for the night, just a little nightlight radiating from the living room. I went back out to the car and brought in the box of money. I locked up and looked at the clock. It was eleven thirty. The best place for the box for the time being was in my closet. I shoved the box way back toward the winter coats and long dresses. It will be safe there, I thought. Pulling off my clothes, I lay down across the bed and in a few minutes I was asleep. It had been a long night and day.

Chapter 10

My grandmother had been in the hospital three weeks and her doctor, Raymond Scott, called and asked if I could come by his office before he released her.

"Yes, of course." I answered. Did you want me to make an appointment, or is it urgent?

"Well, yes and no. If you can get in today, I'd like to talk to you. Can you come in around four o'clock? I should be finished with calls by then. Just tell the girl in the office when you arrive. She can show you in.

"I'll be there at four. Thank you Doctor Scott."

"Your welcome, Lynette, see you then."

I wonder what that was all about. Oh God, something else to worry about, just when the old lady was calming down a bit. I dressed and headed over to the office.

When I was ushered in, Doctor Scott was flipping through a chart. He gestured to the nurse and pointed to a chair across from his desk. Shuffling the papers around in the chart, which I assumed was my grandmother's. He removed his glasses and began speaking. "Lynette, are you aware that your grandmother has a personality problem?" No secret there I thought. He went on, "Has she ever been diagnosed for any mental disorders?"

"Well, she's always been a little weird, but lately I thought she had mellowed out a little."

"After talking with her at length," he began, "I decided to do a PSYC evaluation on her. Lynette, your grandmother has a complicated mental condition. She's seriously schizophrenic, and probably one of the worse cases I've seen in my career. Surely, you've experienced some evidence of her condition."

"Well, yes I have. But I thought she was just getting old and being a little more crazy than usual. She raised us kids, you know. My mother and her sister dumped us off on my grandmother and took off. She took care of us throughout her whole life. Our family life was not like June Cleaver, but we all survived, I guess. What do think we should do, Doctor Scott?"

"I think she should be institutionalized for a while. She can be medicated and maybe helped in a structured environment. She will need to receive some sort of treatment. I recommend that she be monitored at all times. From her responses, if true, she's had everyone in her life on a short leash, possibly committed felonies and endangered others. For your sake and anyone else involved in her life, she needs to be in professional hands. I've had four different doctors examine her; Psychiatrists, two of them, an analyst, and a couple of mental health experts look at her, and each of them prescribed medication and advised that she be kept in secured areas. She's quite intelligent. Her I.Q. is 135, she's no dummy, but the more smarts they have, the closer attention these types of individuals need." Doctor Scott hesitated a full minute, staring out the window, and then back at me.

I wondered if she told him about the money, and what should I say if he asked. I won't say anything. Let him think what he wants. Who could tell whether a crazy woman was making things up or if was true. Doctor Scott went on. "After we can get her to the point where she takes her medicine, we can get her into a nursing home. I think that would be best, but its up to you, Lynette."

"That would be fine with me, Doctor Scott, whatever you say. Listen, I want to thank you for all the help you've given my grandmother."

"Well, Lynette, you've done a lot, and shouldered a heavy responsibility for a long time." He looked me straight in the eyes. "You deserve to live a comfortable life now, and not worry about your grandmother anymore. She will be well taken care of and you can enjoy the rest of your life in peace."

I shook his hand then hugged Doctor Scott. "Thank you, thank you for all you've done."

Coming out of the office, I made the sign of the cross. "Thank God," I said, and I really meant it. I walked slowly toward my parked car and breathing a sigh of relief got in, turned on the ignition and slowly drove toward my Pittsburg home. I put all thoughts of my Grandmother out of my mind. The knowledge of her past is something I don't want to think about ever again. I began to sing again, Oh happy day, Oh happy day. My heart was so light that I felt I could just float away like a balloon toward the outer limits of earth.

It was still early in the day and Pearl was asleep in the recliner, her chin resting on her chest. I went to the closet, drug out the box, brought it into the laundry room and dumped the money into the washer filled with warm water a small amount of tide. After I had laundered the money and dried it, I stacked it into neat little piles and distributed it around to five different banks, earning twelve percent interest. I put the accounts under the various names of my children, and then stopped off at Snooker Pete's for a cold beer. I deserved it.

*Authors note: The story is based on real people and stories that actually happened, but given a little more life through the authors imagination.

THE SAD LUCK STORY OF NUMBER 46.

Martinez, California 1935

A final handshake and bus ticket to the little town of Pleasanton summed up the 20-year stay at Folsom State Prison. His destination was the only other place he remembered besides the enclosed gates, the prison yard and the eight by eight cement cages that he had endured through his youth and into near middle age. There was no place else to go. He had served his time. When the warden asked about what he would do when he left, he hung his head down moved it from side to side. His memories of Pleasanton consisted of four years working for the Hestons and before that, four years at the Napa State Hospital. The boy had been placed there after he had been the lone survivor of an automobile accident that took his parents and five-year-old child who had a serious head injury coupled by traumatic shock that rendered him speechless.

Diagnosed as retarded by the physicians at the County Hospital where he had been taken after the accident in1938, the hospital at Martinez had stitched the lacerated face and scalp and attempted to communicate with the five-year old boy without much success. There was no information on the kid and no one laid claim to him. Any attempt to reach him resulted in a blank expression that indicated to the doctors that the child was damaged beyond help. Child welfare placed him with the other young children who had ended their short lives at Napa State Hospital for the Insane.

Old Tom Dulaney managed both the janitor and the ground maintenance crews in the hospital. He worked from seven in the morning until five o'clock in the afternoon supervising and substituting for those who didn't report on duty for various reasons. The work was tedious and at times frustrating as he worked with the crew, some of who were also handicapped in some way. Many of the workers were castoffs from the world outside of the Asylum, making it even more difficult to maintain an atmosphere that might bring a little peace. Some of the men were abusive and cruel to the inmates and Tom had to intervene with the pushing and shoving of the helpless, yet stubborn patients who might get the worst in a confrontation. The groaning, endless murmuring and screaming of the patients left little patience for any of the people who put in long, dreary hours caring for the poor inmates drooling spittle from unshaven chins and spastic bodies.

Tom Dulaney began to see a light at the end of the tunnel when he had reached sixty-five years old; thirty-five of them spent at the Asylum. He had put in his notice and had just one month to go. But one decision yet to be made was causing many sleepless nights for old Tom, what to do about the boy. Number 46 needed to be saved and he was the only hope. He needed to go before the Hospital Board and ask if he could legally adopt the kid. 46 did not have any folks, and neither did old Tom. He would at least have a chance at life if he could take him along when he walked out of here. At least Tom knew even if the rest of the world did not, that Number 46 did not belong in this hellhole.

Number 46 had been so named because of the coincidence of the move from room 46 in the old County Hospital at Martinez to ward 46 in the Napa State Hospital. In the official charts that were kept, the papers listed the boy as an unknown and he was never given a proper name. Whenever the need for an examination of the boy was required to update the records, the child continued to avoid eye contact with the nurses or doctors. His inability to utter sounds staved off any further probe into his state of mind. The original diagnosis was never altered.

Tom Dulaney was the only person who had found a way to break through the barrier that had kept others at a distance. During a time outdoors in the enclosed area, Tom had observed the boy studying a colony of ants that had formed a single line to an unknown nest. The boy's eyes were focused and intent on what he was seeing. He had found an uneaten crust of jellied bread and had attracted the column of ants to change direction. So intent was the boy's attention as Tom continued to stare at the drama before him that the old man dropped the rake he had been working with. The boy looked quickly around in order to discover the source of the sound. His eyes were alert and focused on the unknown intrusion and before he could cover up his response, the boy's eyes met Tom's, both were surprised at the encounter that had occurred.

At that moment in time, a secret relationship was formed between the old man and the boy. Whenever the two met outdoors, the boy allowed the man to watch his interaction between the wildlife in the yard and at times even allowed a small smile to pass between them. Tom had attempted to talk with one of the doctors on staff about Number 46. The doctor immediately rebuffed his inference of normalcy that conflicted with his opinion and other medical staff workers who had reached a previous diagnosis of retardation.

Ever so slowly, a bond developed between man and child. Tom the watchful caretaker and the boy that had lowered the curtain to everyone but the old man. The simple acts of kindness such as a candy bar slipped under the pillow of Number 46 sealed the secret friendship of the unlikely duo. Both recognized the need to make it a covert relationship and never revealed or jeopardized the bond they had formed over the next five years. Tom's mind began to ponder over different scenarios that would solve the problem of taking Number 46 with him when he retired. Within the month of his retirement, unusual circumstances would dictate a course of action that could not have been imagined in his wildest dreams.

In the boiler room of the hospital a small, undetected gas leak caused a disaster that would be talked about for years after the event. An explosion and subsequent fire destroyed a complete wing of the hospital, engulfing a large portion of the rooms filled with children. A total of 84 deaths resulted and very few escaped the holocaust. The two that did escape were numbered among the lost and presumed dead.

Tom heard the explosion that morning of November 30th, 1943 and with clarity of purpose, despite the ensuing chaos, he ran toward the children's wing. As he entered the smoke-filled hallway, he quickly grabbed Number 46 and urgently propelled him towards the locked gates. The parking area and garage that stood behind the hospital gave them the coverage needed to pull out the old Ford truck and avoid the sirens that were blasting away in an effort to reach the conflagration. Fire trucks and ambulances converged at the gates of the Asylum as Tom and boy sped out of the back exit, avoiding detection.

Tom's living quarters above a garage had an alleyway in back of the garage so that the pair could gain entrance to the apartment without being seen. Fate had entered into the dilemma that had faced Tom. Now his worries were over about how he could get the boy out of the

Asylum. It would probably be safe to spend the night at the apartment and then take off for the farm in Livermore in the morning.

The farm had been left to Tom as the older members of the family had passed on. He and the boy could start a new life together. Only a few clothes were taken from his room so as not to arouse suspicion from the landlord. The assumption that the fire had taken his tenant would probably be accepted by anyone who might inquire about him. No one would be looking for either of them and Tom felt that somebody up there was directing the whole show. When Tom and Number 46 arrived at the farm, it was three o'clock in the morning. The isolated location of the old farm allowed them to quietly fit into the small community. The little nest egg of savings that Tom had squirreled away over years was enough to begin the new life that both had deserved.

Number 46 was nine years old and had no memories of anyplace other than the institution that had shaped him. It was a difficult transition to be torn from the bedlam of the noisy Asylum to begin a new life on the quiet house with acres of land surrounding them, but in the course of time, small incremental changes took place. Tom's quiet good humor and constant praise took its desired effect as Number 46 adapted to the life in Livermore. A new name was chosen by Tom and approved by the boy now referred to as Jimmy.

Life could not be sweeter when the Heston family hired Tom to work on a small farm, tending cattle. Jimmy came along and was paid a minimal wage working alongside his mentor. Lyle Heston had one son named Wayne. His wife had died giving birth to Wayne, and the years of loneliness caused him to frequent the bars to bring surcease to the emptiness he felt. Years later, when Wayne was sixteen, Lyle met and subsequently married a young tart from Monterey named Rose. Within a year, Rose became increasingly bored with the marriage and Lyle soon lost interest in her because of the constant nagging about his work and lack of energy to perform in bed. He complained to Tom about his bad luck in taking on a marriage to someone young enough to be his daughter. What an old fool he was! "Nothing good will come of it", he said, not once, but again and again as he lamented his fate.

Rose began to playfully tease young seventeen-year old Wayne and flirted outrageously in front of Lyle until she got some kind of reaction which usually resulted in Lyle taking off and spending more time in the Livermore Saloon than at home after he had finished his work. Wayne, pimple-faced and gangly with the typical teenage urges for affection and approval, began to respond to Rose's overt suggestive comments. As expected by all that had observed the melodrama being played out, the son and the wife began a sordid affair that became grist for the scandalmongers of the town.

One evening, and bits of barroom gossip was being bantered about. Lyle caught wind of the talk that his wife was playing around. Even though he had suspected her for sometime, he had to put on a show to mark his regard for his reputation. He stomped out of the bar after more than a few shots of whiskey and drove home to see the bare ass of a man jumping out of the door to his balcony. They had heard the car door slam and Lyle spotted the man as he threw himself over the banister and dropped to the ground below. Lyle bolted upstairs to the bedroom, grabbed Rose and struck her several time with his fist. "Who was the man you had in bed with you", he demanded to know. Rose knew that if he suspected that it was Wayne, Lyle would surely kill her. "It was the dummy, he raped me", she said. Lyle sunk down to his knees and vomited up the last few hours of liquor and peanuts. "My God, get out of my house this minute before I kill you", he shouted.

Tom routed Jimmy out of bed when Lyle came over with a shotgun, promising to blow Jimmy's brains out. The police were called after Tom had calmed him down a bit, and Jimmy was taken in for questioning. Rose was also brought in and questioned as to the veracity of her accusations. Again and again, she never strayed from her story of Jimmy coming into the bedroom and raping her. Jimmy was arraigned for trial and subsequently sentenced to twenty years in Folsum Prison. Tom had suffered a massive heart attack when Jimmy had been arrested for rape. There was no one to defend the mute who had reverted to hanging his head down and turning it from side to side. Eyes that no longer held any look other than a blank expression of helplessness.

After Jimmy's incarceration the years took on a surrealistic tone. Time passed and Number 46 slowly began to respond to his environment, to learn the ropes and how to avoid confrontation with the other inmates. He was tested by the prison psychiatrist and found to have aphasia, but diagnosed as having above normal intelligence. He obediently worked in the kitchen and taught himself to read and write. Jimmy Dulaney had at last found himself and before his release, contacted Wayne Heston who had been his only friend. Wayne, now married, had inherited the farm from his father and had lived with the guilt of his affair with Rose. Years passed and as his father lay dying, Wayne confessed that he was the one who had been with Rose that night, now had the chance to redeem himself by asking Jimmy to come to work for him. As the bus driver called out the next stop, Jimmy bent over and picked up his suitcase and began to step down off the bus. He stumbled as he recognized the middle-aged woman seated on the bench, a disheveled and shopworn Rose Heston. Her hair was tangled, a smear of lipstick on the mouth, jaws clenched in a hard line. Old before her time, eyes blank and unfocused as she sits, waiting for the time to pass when she can go home to a lonely rented room in the back of the Livermore saloon.

Although the small town of Antioch was named for a famous city in Turkey, the southern tip of the capitol of the ancient kingdom of Syria, it has had it's own unique history of the famous and infamous, making its mark in colorful stories of its early day citizens.

CRIMES AND PUNISHMENT

The following information is resurrected from an old piece of writing, edited and rewritten by Marti Aiello. Although the small town of Antioch was named for a famous city in Turkey, the southern tip of the capitol of the ancient kingdom of Syria, it has had its own unique history of the famous and infamous, making its mark in colorful stories of its early day citizens.

A Short Christmas Story

It was a cold, clear night on December 21 of 1866 when William Nesbit decided to mend fences and resolve difference between himself and George Vernon who lived in a little town of Somersville, located a few miles from his home near Antioch. Nesbit may have been a little guilt-ridden and it being near the season of Christmas, he would do his part to make amends. As he approached Vernon's house, he explained that with Christmas coming, it would be a good time to bury the hatchet so to speak, and make peace with his old neighbor. George agreed and went into the house, picked up a pistol and came out onto the porch. Bill had been sitting there musing how nice it would be to make an enemy a friend when George came out and shot him in the chest. Nesbit took off running and received sever other shots in the back. Though it wasn't the kind of peace he asked for or deserved, he was buried in the Roseville cemetery and Vernon was charged with manslaughter and ended up in jail for 10 years. Governor Haight rescinded the order declaring, "There were serious doubts as to his guilt", and pardoned him.

He must have had a very good lawyer.

CRIMES AND PUNISHMENT

You might think the following storyline was taken from an old-time flick, replete with nefarious character, victims, bad guys (and gals), sheriffs, barkeepers, and assorted felons. As a matter of fact, it would make a fine old-time movie, piano playing in the background as cards are dealt around a felt-covered round table. The setting was a rooming house in the coal town of Somersville, a small burg in the hills above the nearby town of Smith's Landing (now the site of the city of Antioch).

It was on February 20, 1867 when William Bowen and Enock J. Davis got into an argument over a card game. The Barkeep ordered the two men outside to settle their differences. During the course of the argument, comments being traded back and forth between the two men, Davis made remarks on the marital status of Bowen's parents. Davis stood with his hands on his hips, nose almost touching Bowen's beak while he spewed a few more cutting remarks, aggravating Bowen to the point where he drew a knife and plunged the deadly weapon into the chest of his adversary.

Davis slipped to the floor after the deadly assault, blood oozing rapidly from the blow to his heart. However, the blow was not fatal. Davis lingered a few more days and it was thought that he would recover. His chest was wrapped tight in a torn sheet and he was carried to a room at the Cumberland house owned by Davis. A mid-wife called "Granny Norton", who serviced both the town of Nortonville and Somersville, was called into tend to the injured man. After examining the wound, Granny opined that she could do nothing for the man and moved on to take care of more pressing issues that caring for another boozing scoundrel with a penchant for fighting. Davis died a few days later, and was buried on the hill in the Rose Hill Cemetery and life went on as before.

It is not known whether a lawman was called in to talk with Bowen about the murder and in a few years time, it was history. A telling footnote to the fact that life wasn't worth a plug nickel in those days.

Lizzy Borden took and ax and gave her husband forty whacks

And when she found that he was 'done', she gave another forty-one.

A few years pass, and on November 16, 1872 the body of Valentine Eischler was found near Marsh Creek. For a small community the size of Somersville, it seems a lot of unusual "happenings" kept the residents entertained with some "goings on" that might surprise the most sophisticated readers in this twenty-first century.

It seems that Eischiler, poor man, was married to a woman who didn't think nearly as much about him as she did such worldly goods as might accrue to a widow. The Eischiler's had hired a man named Marshall Martin who was nuts bout the lady, or maybe just plain nuts.

Anyway, she talked him into going into Antioch and obtaining a quantity of arsenic that she mixed in some stewed pumpkin, home grown in her backyard garden. Now it appears that Mr. Eischler did not care for stewed pumpkin, and after sitting a couple of days in the icebox Mrs. E. poured it down the privy. A couple more days passed when she made up a dish, liberally spiked with arsenic and it too was passed on. Well, this wasn't working as well as she hoped. She got a second chance when Fischler said he was going to drive out to Point of Timber and buy some pigs. This suited his wife very well and she prepared a favorite for the dear man. You guessed it, a bottle of whiskey laced with arsenic.

As fate would have it, Eischler decided he would not drink that day and arrived home as hale and hearty as ever. A more aggressive plan was adopted that seemed like a sure thing. Martin would shove his boss out of the buggy as they drove through the canyons on the way to town. But then, luck was on the side of the innocent, and Eischler was asked by a neighbor to allow him to go along for the ride, and the scheme went up in smoke.

An elaborate plot was constructed when Martin decided to shoot the man, but when he couldn't find any shells for the gun he needed to go all the way to Vallejo to buy some. Mrs. E. was asked for the cash for the ammunition and the plan was put in action. Everything was set when Eischler and Martin were sent to Antioch for flour. Martin had the gun, which was covered with a blanket. Eischler bid his wife adieu, climbed into the wagon with Martin and took off down the hill,

When the two men drew close to the house, Mrs. Eischler saw Mr. E. alive and well, sitting cozily with her lover, Martin, she exploded. Puzzled by her outburst, Mr. Eiscler returned the anger with his response to her outrage of finding him still alive. "Woman, take your clothes and go back to the whorehouse where you came from"

Well, that did it! She picked up an ax and said, "I'll give you a whorehouse" and gave him 40 whacks on the head, and for luck, she gave him a couple more.

The deed done, she called Martin to come and drag the body into the stable. After this, Martin saddled his; horse and told Mrs. E. that he was going over to the Good Templar's Lodge at the Eden Schoolhouse. Mrs. E. told him that he should tell the people that Eishler had been kicked to death by a horse.

The following day, neighbors came to pay their respects and were amazed that the body of Mr. Eischler had already been laid to rest, and put in an unmarked grave. Well, it seemed too strange a story to be believed and Martin and his partner in crime was hauled off to the lock-up in Antioch and charge with murder.

On January 23, 1875, Marshall Martin, was sentenced to be hanged by the neck until dead and Mrs. E. was sent off to the booby hatch in Stockton where she spent the rest of her miserable life. It seems that just about everybody got their just deserts.

In nearby Sidney Flat, a number of establishments described as entertainment and recreational halls (saloons) provided a place for the young or unattached men to gather. Music and woman drew them into the two-story hotel where they could drink and visit the ladies of the night all in one evening's fun and frolic joint. A visiting gentleman named Mr. Green was escorting a handsome young woman named "Hattie", one of the ladies who worked at the dance hall, home. She might have been in one of her "bad moods", because she began to cry and carry on and refused to go with him. To the rescue came James Carroll who told her escort that she sure as hell didn't need Green to force her to go home with him, though he may have paid in advance, she had a right to change her mind.

To add to the night's entertainment, one young man following the three ahead of him began to play a musical piece on a toy harmonica, and behind him, a young man with a bottle of whiskey provided the lyrics to the music in a fine tenor voice adding to the melodic sounds of the night. James Carroll apparently was not a music affettuoso and did not appreciate the accompanying contributions of the pair, grabbed the booze away from the young man and shot the tenor dead. For his bad judgment of the musical rendition, the court sentenced him to 20 years in the Stony Lonesome.

It was a dark and stormy night of February 1, 1868 in nearby Antioch. The wind was howling and whipping up the brush that grew in tuffs around Dahnkens' Saloon, when Bill Brunkhouse stumbled through the bar on his way to the back room of the establishment. He was assisted by George Mitchell a paid employee hired to keep the peace at the bar. He bid Bill goodnight, mentioning "that it was not a fit night for man nor beast to be out in this kinda weather." Mitchell headed back to the bar and Carson Dahnken, the proprietor, had already closed the place and didn't notice if George came back. Later, those patrons too drunk to care or others trying to make it home before the wife locked the door had attested to hearing a pistol shot accompanied by the sound of breaking glass. Nobody bother to investigate.

The next morning, George had not made an appearance at the bar and Dahnken began to wonder about his whereabouts until a patron noticed a trail of blood leading to the wharf where a body was found, face down and limp. A top hat floating nearby, looking suspiciously like the one George always wore, aroused Dahnken to call the coppers. Suspects were rounded up. One, a sailor pointing fingers at William Hank who was a skipper of the schooner, the "A.P. Jordan", which was anchored a little ways downstream.

Hank, a belligerent, angry drunk had been barhopping around town, drinking heavily and waving a pistol around, challenging fellow customers at Martin's Saloon. He had been restrained several times that day and continued to binge on booze until evening when he went into Gordon's Saloon and told the bartender there that he had shot a man. The bartender, dealing with drunks and miscreants nearly all the time, told him to go home and sleep it off. Hank left the bar and spent some time out in the street shooting at dogs that freely roamed the streets of the town looking for garbage to eat.

Finally, at the end of the day, Hank staggered into a hotel and broke into the room of a guest, Joseph Parker, and demanded a bed to sleep in. Instead Parker led him into the hotel lobby where he stretched out on a sofa and fell asleep, dropping his pistol to the floor.

By the time George Mitchell's body was found, the story of the drunken sailor with a mean streak had circulated around and back to the constable serving Antioch. Constable Pitts tracked to the schooner that had taken Hank on Board and headed for the open seas.

When Hanks had seen trouble coming in the guise of Constable Pitts, he jumped into the water and tried to get away. After a bit of a struggle, Hanks was hauled out of the water and brought back to the courts where he was tried and acquitted. He didn't quite escape punishment though, for after the trial he was married to a Miss Myrtle Augusta Rayner of Antioch. She was well known, loud-mouthed "Harpy" that hung around the numerous bars of the small town that had attracted sailors who had dropped anchor at the harbor.

We don't know the outcome of Hank's marriage, but we can only hope it was a fitting punishment for this gun-toting drunken sailor.

*   *   *

THE HILLS of HOME

Chapter 1

My mother hated it, the place where we lived. I thought it was beautiful. A meandering dirt road, not more than twenty or thirty feet between the ditches that ran parallel to the road carried the water away when it rained. We lived in the valley between the two hills and we either walked uphill or downhill. There was not a level place in the two-mile road that brought us in or out of the valley. It was also known as, "Cow Shit Hollow". The neighborhood from the S curved bend to the top of the hill where the Fisher's lived was approximately an eight of a mile. The Namack family lived on the left hand side of the curve in a single storied hovel that had never seen a coat of paint. The Namack family had all boys, Carl Jr., called Tubby, Lester, called Buddy and Eugene, called Puchie. Roy Miller and his wife Evelyn and son, Roy Junior, lived next door in a nice four-room house, painted white with green trim. Our house was the third one up the hill. It had started out as a one-storied, peaked roof with a living, dining and kitchen downstairs.

The beds were lined up under the eaves of the second level. Later my Dad and some neighbors raised the roof, and the house took on the appearance of a barn. We came upstairs through a narrow staircase. Hollyhocks grew up to the roof and I could squeeze out of the small window and pick them. My girl friend, Margaret, and I created stick dolls and dressed them in the flower of the hollyhocks. Of course, they didn't last long, and when they wilted, we picked some more. We also picked the wild violets that appeared in the spring and I put them in a small milk bottle filled with water and placed them on my dresser in the bedroom. My brothers, Bill and Jack slept in one room and me in another with a doll named Shirley.

Down the hill near the curve in the road was a well that someone had built along time ago. It was about two foot round and made of brick. It caught the underground water that coursed through the hills and came out of a copper spout that dropped into the well. It was the sweetest water I have ever tasted and it was something I missed when I moved away. When I was very young, I would wait near the well with a couple of buckets and as soon as I saw Dad coming up the hill from work, I would signal him with the message that Mom needed water. As my brothers and I grew older, it was our job to carry the fresh drinking water up to the house.

There was a cellar that Dad had built when he made the foundation of our house. We entered the cellar by pulling on a ring in the floor to raise a six-foot section of it up and then used the side of the wall to rest it on. It was where my mother did the laundry. The water in the cistern was about six feet deep and was carried in via the waterspouts coming from the rooftops that drained the rain off of the slanted roof. Water was heated in a big copper kettle over a wood-burning stove. When the washing machine was filled up to the brim, we poured in the soap and added the dirty clothes. The old Maytag washer swished to the right and left for hours on end in the process of cleaning the mountains of dirty clothes we generated every week. When I was a little older my mother allowed me to run the clothes through the ringer of the washer. It was a kind of dangerous job as the clothes were pushed through two round padded pieces that went round as you wound it with a handle. If you didn't get your finger out fast enough your hand could be caught in the ringer. This happened only once if you were smart.

Mom also did the canning of jams and jellies down in the basement. The cellar was cool and I didn't mind helping Mom in the heat of the hot summer. About mid-month in September we had a mountain of black coal delivered to the yard of our house. We kids were employed by Dad to carry tin buckets of coal to the chute that emptied into the basement and used to heat the furnace that kept us warm during the cold weather seasons. It was hard work and took us most of one day to get the coal into the cellar. At the end of the day, the coal dust had been transferred to every inch of our now blackened bodies. Mom would not ever let us near the door to the house. Water was brought out and cups used to quench out thirst. We were hosed off periodically to eat a sandwich at lunchtime and we looked like raccoons by the end of day. My dad worked hardest of all. He had a shovel in his hand and kept our buckets full as we ran back and forth from the yard to the coal chute. Dad judged the amount of work we did by seeing how much dirt covered our bodies. It was just another job that we were expected to do and we felt like an important part of the family of workers that took pride in out ability to perform such a task. Mom put the old tin tub out in the front yard and at the end of the day, Dad scrubbed our bodies with a bar of yellow laundry soap and scooped up clean water to rinse the dirt off. Mom laid out clean shorts and tops on the swing and we dressed there on the porch.

The cellar was truly the heart of our house. In the fall of the year my Dad made various spirits. Keep in mind that this was in the days of prohibition and West Virginia was a dry state. My father was a kind of chemist, mixing, fermenting grapes, elderberries and hops to make wine, beer and whiskey. At Christmas time, he would distribute the bottles to family members as gifts. It took him a few years to catch my brothers at helping themselves to the stock on hand. Both Billy and Jackie had tapped the bottles and the keg. Later when they tried to lay down to sleep it off, the spinning room caused them to puke and to add insult to injury, Dad got out his razor strap and asked the boys to bent over for a much deserved licking. Mom had always been the disciplinarian in the family and when Dad got out his razor strap and whipped the boys behind, this was a big deal.

Our house was set back from a sloped yard and six steps led us downward to the cement floor of the porch that extended out about ten feet from the house. We had a swing that was hooked up to the ceiling of the porch. Mom loved to sit there in the summer evenings and sing the old songs that she had heard from the music of the 1920's. Some of the songs that I remember told a story; one in particular that I could sing even to this day. At times, I would lay my head in her lap while she brushed and braided my hair. My mother was both strict and yet soft at times. When she was out of sorts, we kids could be on the short end of the palm of her hand.

At my mother's insistence, Dad built a bathroom inside. That was great, but we did not have indoor plumbing for years. A tin pail kept filled with water was used to flush the toilet. We needed to carry water in from the outside pump, heat it in a large copper kettle and fill the footed tub. Every Saturday evening we had a bath. My mother filled a tin tub in the warm kitchen for us kids and since I was a girl, she let me go first. By the time my younger brother, Jackie got in the water, the soap scum was evident, but he never complained. Dumb kid! Later on, when I was about ten, my mother let me bathe in the large tub.

We had an outhouse about twelve feet from the house. The one-seat, lidded hole was almost over the small "crick" that ran from the top of our hill to the twenty-ninth Street culvert. We had a small bridge over the "run" that linked us to the tool shed that Daddy had built and later became my playhouse. Further down the hill, kids played in the creek and hunted crawdads. I guess nobody told them about our placement of the outhouse. And I wasn't about to break the news.

Bill was two years older than me, and my brother Jack, two years younger. My mother really liked him the best. He had everybody charmed. It caused a lot of rivalry between the two of us, and me being the middle kid, I had to fight for my place in the family. In thinking back, I guess I was a little hard on Jackie, and he was a born fighter, trying to establish his place in the family. I feel I may have been responsible for his reputation later as one of the best street fighters in the neighborhood. Nobody could push my brother Jackie around when 'charm' didn't work.

The old man and woman who lived next door to us, was Aunt Mandy and Pappy. Not related to us, but the neighbor who took care of us when my parents left for work. I just remembered a small house with a porch swing where Mandy and Pappy spent their time. The Atkinson's lived next door to Aunt Mandy. Betty and Ray were the kids I played with and Edith Atkinson was my mother's friend. The house next door to them was empty. It was an extremely big two-story house painted white. Some of the windows had been broken, and the door was forever ajar. According to Pud Shaffer, it was haunted. Only the very brave ventured in, and when we did, we tiptoed up the winding staircase about halfway and screamed as our bravado waned and we went flying down the stairs and out the door.

The Shaffer's lived across from my house and next to them, the Auten's. My Friend, Gracie and her brother, Thomas Auten, were part of the neighborhood gang. Unlike my other friends whose homes were always open, we had never set foot in Gracie's home. All of the windows were covered with dark canvas blinds at all times and her Mother and Gracie's big sister, Eleanor, stayed inside always. I don't ever remember seeing a father, but they talked about him as if he also lived there.

The Schocksnyders, a German couple who owned a bakery somewhere on the "Pike" and a pretty, curly-haired girl of my age named Shirley lived in a lovely large white house with a picket fence that encircled the property that was guarded by a large dog. I was the only one in the neighborhood who could come in and play with Shirley. I think it was because I was polite and so happy to be in the beautiful house, and I had a German last name. It was Lautenschlager. My first name was Myrtle. The middle name was Marlyn Etta. And when I first attended the school down on Twenty-ninth Street, the kids in my class would snicker when my name was announced. This incident, so early in my career, intensified my desire to leave the hill and change my name, which I did, but not until I was twelve years old. Beyond the Schocksnyders were the Fisher's. Margaret was my best friend and her cousin, was my first love. On a warm summer night, he climbed the rose trellis and crawled onto the roof and we kissed through the screened-in window. I will always remember Phillip Walker. He was quite good looking, with dark hair and blue eyes. He was well behaved and a little shy. The folks who I described were all part of my world.

We lived on one of the many hills that were part of the Appalachian Mountain range, in the panhandle of West Virginia. The freedom-loving wildness of the place where I lived was as much a part of me as the abundance of trees and growing things that dotted the landscape that surrounded me. Story had it that the famed "Johnny Appleseed" had come though our land and planted the seeds of apple and pears and peaches throughout the hills where we lived. In the spring of the year, the blossoms of pink and white stood out like flowers among the green boughs of the trees as thick as you can imagine. As long as the season of spring to fall, I felt sheltered by the trees as I made my way up the hill alone to sit in the flat green spot at the top; this place where I could lay among the wild flowers and look up through the puffy white clouds and see if I could find the place where God lived.

The heat of summertime was as fierce as the deep snows of winter. But summertime was my favorite time of year. It was hot and muggy, drops of sweat streaked my tanned and dusty body as the sun stayed overhead and beat down on the fair skin of my brothers. Both boys were blue-eyed, fair-haired and rosy-white as an Irish ancestor gladly shared the genes of the heredity of Ireland or the blond youths of Southern Germany. In turn, the white skin burned a hot pink when exposed, whereas mine turned a shade or two darker. Whatever the reason for the differences in our appearances and disposition, it was obvious I did not resemble either of my folks. Even my eyes were not the familiar blue of my ancestors, but a smoky gray, cat's eyes, as my mother described them. She also called them 'China eyes'. Not quite the usual, but acceptable enough if you happened to be a cat. I didn't mind though, these eyes could sparkle or turn fierce in the heat of anger. I could outstare anyone I faced and they would be sure to look away. My hair and brows, originally light, turned a non-descript brown very early, and I think I was put together nicely.

During the summer, swimming was on the mind of the kids lucky enough to live on our hill. The trek to one of the tributaries of the Ohio River was a two-mile hike. We gathered together and walked single-file up the hill, across a valley and then down toward the water. Each of us carried a rag dishtowel full of jelly sandwiches and apples or pears from our yard. If we passed by a farm, we helped ourselves to any fruit tree that we spied. We might expect the farmer to yell at us from his house or yard if he saw us. It made the stealing twice worth the fun of picking from a stranger's property. When we reached the hill above the river below us, our spirits rose with anticipation of our hot sweating bodies being cooled by the water coming from the many springs that ran underground then coursed over the rocks and into the gulches that ran between the hills. Finally, we were there at Wheeling Creek, and we watched with fascination as water moccasins slithered along the limbs of the trees that hung over the water just a few feet away.

As soon as we spied the water below, we let out a whoop and a holler and slid down the slippery, muddy slope toward the small stony dry riverbed that ran parallel to the river. We dropped our bundles and quickly pulled off our clothes and stripped to our underpants before running into the cold water; screaming when our hot bodies unexpectedly met the cold shower of splashing bodies disturbing the water. After we had our fill, we limped ashore over the stony pebbles along the sandy beach, reaching for our bag lunches and hurriedly emptying the contents. We lay on the small grassy patches and starred at the blue summer skies until the sun reached about three o'clock and then we packed up and started our return trek homeward. Our bodies once more bathed in sweat, causing hair and clothing to dampen so that we quickly stripped to our waist to feel again the airless heat. After an hour and a half of walking, we reached the top of our hill to see the rooftops of our houses baking in the afternoon sun. As we parted, the Namack boys ran the last half-mile toward home so as to be there before their father came from work. Neither me, nor my brothers cared about that. My parents came home later and Daddy would get out his bugle and play retreat when he wanted us home for dinner or he would play taps if we were to come home at bedtime. These were very strict rules set out and understood. Disobedience was not tolerated.

The last few weeks of summer brought the lush blackberries in season. My mother baked blackberry pies and made jam with the rest. My brothers and me worked tirelessly to provide the fruit that was changed into a delicious dessert or a spread for the homemade bread Mama baked. We would be up early in the morning to find a berry patch loaded with enough fruit to fill a lard can. After we had picked enough for my mother, we would go through the neighborhood selling the berries for 25 cents a bucket. It seemed that the whole world opened itself to the joy of a walk through the woods or a summer swim and also ways to earn a little money for a movie now and then.

Chapter 2

On Saturday afternoon, we got cleaned up. My brothers in overalls of jean material and me in cotton dress and scuffed up shoes. We met up with the other kids of the neighborhood and together we walked all the way down to 29th Street, then down to the Southern Theater where we watched the cowboy movies of the 1930's. Roy Rogers rescued every damsel in distress, as did Nelson Eddy of the Royal Canadian Mounties, who would invariably end up singing to Jeanette McDonald. We sat through a double feature, two or three cartoons and the Pathe News. Buck Rodgers, the hero who traveled through time, was a series that ran week after week and we tried not to miss any. The time for the going and coming from the movies, and the show itself took about five hours. By that time the sun had set and the early shadows moved in stillness as we climbed up the tree-studded hills. The hair on the back of my neck raised and fear and anxiety overtook me as the boys ran ahead and hid behind a tree, then ran out with hands raised to scare the shit out of me. Just walking along and seeing the trees rustling in the breeze caused me to wet my pants in fear. I might have been seven or eight at the time and still insecure in the darkness of the summer nights. Yet, I would never turn down the chance to go through it all again, Saturday after Saturday as long as the weather allowed.

Other entertainment that filled our nights was listening and staring at the radio. My parents were one for rituals. For example, on Saturdays, my Dad cooked lunch and it was always fried liver and onions and mashed potatoes. It didn't make any difference to my Dad if we moaned and groaned over the fact that every one of us kids hated . . . I mean really hated, liver. The problem was if we didn't eat the liver, we did not have a choice of any other food. Liver was on the plate next to the mashed potatoes. As much as we moved the liver around the plate, it did not disappear and we could not leave the table until the plate was empty. Most of the time, if my parent's attention was directed on each other in conversation, the liver was dropped into my lap and transferred to a pocket until the meal was over and my plate clean. My father went on and on about the value of building bodies by eating the right kind of food, he meant liver. Even though we lived in 1930's, the time of the great depression, we never went hungry, and I never thought of myself as poor. We talked about others who were poor and my mother never passed a panhandler without dropping in a few pennies or a nickel. Whenever my Dad mentioned the poor people who would have given an arm or leg to have a meal like liver, I offered my plate up for the cause. My father just glared at me and my mother giggled.

My parents did not attend church or speak of God or the Angels that I had seen pictures of in some book. Although I did have a painting that hung over my bed, that of a young child crossing a bridge and an angel looking down from the sky. It made me feel safe and comforted. But, we as a family did not attend church. So when asked, I tagged along on Sunday morning with the other kids, climbing up the hill and then taking the wagon trail down the rugged path to attend Saint Matthews Episcopalian Church nearby, just blocks away from the bottom of the hill. It was a large cathedral with a very high ceiling and an altar where the priest, dressed in a white gown, climbed up to a pulpit to preach the gospel. We had Sunday school and colored pictures of baby Jesus in the manger with the sheep and oxen. We had to speak very softly and pretend to be very good or the teacher would look at us with mean black eyes. The best part of all was after Thanksgiving and near Christmas when we were each given a box of candy for being good the rest of the year. After this time, the snow was so deep and the path was so hard to follow that we could not go to church again until spring. I will never forget the time we had run into a gigantic snake that lay across our path one Sunday. We screamed and called on the Saints of God to make it disappear. When it finally did, we called it a "miracle' as we related our story to our parents, increasing the size and ferociousness of the monster snake in each telling.

One Sunday I went into a Catholic church and sat next to a very old lady.

Who wore a close fitting hat with a feather on one side. She was kneeling on the wooden narrow strip which folded up with just a kick of the of toe. I tried to emulate her as she made the 'sign of the cross'. Her finger went into a basin of water that sat on a pedestal.

I followed her lead as she touched her forehead with her wet finger. But from then on my hands went from chest to head to right shoulder to belly and I was lost in the process. The woman gently guided my hand a couple of times until I corrected my gesture properly. The memory of the kindness of the woman comes to mind occasionally as I recall those people who showed such mercy to me.

Often on Sundays after church, my dad and mother would take us to visit my great Grandmother Hanke who lived in Benwood, a few miles to the south of Wheeling. Her old two-story house was located on First Street at the end of the block facing the river. The railroad cars ran back and forth in front of the house, dropping coal along the way. It was our job to pick up the coal in buckets and take them to the basement for use later in the winter months. On the other side of the narrow railroad line was a riverbank that held back the Ohio Valley River. It was where my mother had lived as a child. Grandmother Hanke had raised my mother and my Aunt Virginia. Family history has it that my Grandfather William McClellan had married Rosella Marie Delaney, the daughter of a wealthy man who owned a Studebaker car dealership. When she had bore him two daughters, she turned them over to Grandmother Hanke and divorced him. My mother met Rosella when she herself was married and an adult. Grandfather McClellan was an only child of a Scotsman, Jock McClellan of Edinborough. Apparently, he was a sailor in the British Navy under Queen Victoria. He came to America and married my great grandmother, Mary Margaret McCleod. Unfortunately, he was killed in an industrial accident at Wheeling Steel soon after the birth of my grandfather. Her second husband was named Hanke. I only knew him as an old man who smoked a pipe and sat in the rocking chair by the coal stove. When I was in the room, he grumbled and swore, so I would run upstairs to play in the bedroom where this huge bed and dark wardrobe and dresser took up most of the space in the big room.

Every spring, my mother worried about whether my grandmother's house would flood. When it did, and it was often, they would move everything upstairs until the water subsided and they could move back in. My mother would come down to help with the cleanup and to repaper the rooms that had been damaged by the flood. It was the reason that my parents decided to move to the hills and escape the spring flood that was part of the facts of life in the City. I remember coming down off the hill and meeting with my girl friend,

Mary Kay Collette, a classmate of mine from school. We sloshed through the streets in our knee-high boots to see the destruction first hand. Refuse floated on the water and we collected whatever interested us at the time. One Saturday foray into the flooded streets caught me off guard as I walked a little too close to a building and fell into a flooded basement. The grate that covered the opening had been pushed up by the force of the water and I flounder about until some passerby pulled me out as I bubbled to the to the surface, totally immersed, cold and shivering. We knocked on the door of a house nearby and asked to be allowed to change clothes and dry off before I caught pneumonia or died from the freezing water. Several beautiful women were dressed in satin robes, faces painted heavily with rouge and lipstick. Most had blond frizzy hair and looked like movie stars. They were so nice. They undressed me and wrapped me in perfumed robes and gave me a little watered down whiskey to drink to "take away the chill". They called me 'honey' and 'dear' and I felt like I had walked onto a movie set to star in the next film at the Southern Theater, just like Shirley Temple. I had never felt so important. Later, after I had been fed and pampered, I was allowed to go home with Mary Kay at my side. Thoroughly dried, the ladies began to lose interest in me and I couldn't wait to go home and tell my mother what had happened. When we did arrive home, my mother and Dad heard our story about the fall into the flooded basement, and Mama rolled her eyes at Daddy and told us to go to bed. Later, when everyone was down for the night, I heard them talking, something about the house where I had been taken to, whispered in words I had never heard before. When we went to Grandma's house on the next visit, everyone talked about the women who had taken me in when I fell in the water. Again, their eyes met in a silent exchange of information, and it wasn't until much later when I had almost forgotten the episode that I really understood how the ladies made their living. My uncles snickered as they gathered around the round kitchen table and drank small tumblers of whisky, straight.

Grandmother Mcleod was born 1864 and grew up in the mountainous territory of the Appalachia. The region included seven states in the northeastern and the northwestern parts of America and into West Virginia and Pennsylvania. One summer, my Dad took us all in a new 1937 Chevy on a trip to visit her 'kin folks', who lived up in the high hills of West Virginia. We were packed in tight in as we sat in the back seat that held three kids and the rather rounded bottom of my Grandma Hanke who directed my father up a mountainous dirt road that wound around and around the hills in an upward spiral to the place where my great grandmother was born. The man and woman who owned the rustic homestead were my great grandmother's sister and brother-in-law. Their names were Amos and Hattie Larkey. My great aunt Hattie had mixed up a batch of dough and was beating it with her fists when we came through the door. She embraced her sister and welcomed us all with a big hug. The flour had been transferred to each of us as she demonstrated her joy at having 'company'. We were hungry and tired after our long trip and it was late afternoon when we arrived. Aunt Hattie excused herself as she put the dough into the bread pans and lifted them with a wooden pallet into the oven alongside of the fireplace. The aroma of the dampened dirt floor and the soup kettle's contents as well as the baking bread overwhelmed me with the hunger I felt. My brothers had left the house and was chasing each other around the trees and I soon joined them after my aunt had given me a piece of toasted bread and jam to placate the pain in my belly

I remember to this day, a small house with a dirt floor and a large fireplace that dominated the room that was the living area and kitchen combined. An elongated table made of a slab of a tree looked as if it had been honed down with a carving knife. Benches lined both sides. A cauldron of soup hung over the open fire and the smoke swirled up the stone chimney. A round well with a tin bucket hung outside was used to bring up water for drinking and such. An outdoor shithouse was centered over a running stream and we lined up to visit it after we had viewed the house. I asked my mother where we would sleep tonight. She shrugged her shoulders and whispered, "This ain't no hotel." Well, I sure as shootin' knew that much, but hoped it wouldn't be outside. Around the entire area was a forest of very tall trees that had shaded the place and only a slight sunbeam penetrated the shadowy place where the house stood.

After dinner, we were shown the place where we would sleep. We climbed up a ladder to the upstairs. Broad planks were covered with a braided rug-laden floor that was a kind of an open attic. We could look over the edge and see the entire room downstairs. Three straw-covered mattresses were laid side-by-side and covered with quilts. These were our beds, and this was where we would sleep we were told. My dad and mother looked at one another with raised eyebrows. "This is not a hotel", my dad whispered and laughed quietly. During the night I heard the rustle of the straw as mice raced across the floor. The next morning we woke early to the crowing of a rooster. While my parents slept, we kids dressed and climbed down the ladder and ran out the door to the outhouse. My brothers never bothered to use the toilet but bet on which of the two could piss across the creek to the other side. After a nights rest, we were ready to explore the area. A hen house with cackling chickens and geese ran around the yard as we approached. Two penned-up pigs grunted a good-morning as Uncle Amos fed them some slop from last evening's meal. He also grunted a greeting and promised the boys that he would take them hunting later. "I want to go too," I exclaimed. "Girls don't go huntin', yor business is hepin' in the kitchen." I was told.

By the third day of our visit, I was more than ready to go back home, and from the looks of my Dad, so was he. Although it is a memory I will carry with me forever, I can't say that it would be the place where I would like to live.

As we traveled north again toward the panhandle of West Virginia, we no longer stretched our necks to see the passing sights, but was satisfied to rest our eyes in sleep and hear the murmur of our parents and grandma Hanke as our car rumbled along the highway toward home. It was good to be back in familiar surroundings. We had dropped off our grandmother and by that time we kids were asleep. I heard my brother Bill slam the car door and Dad leaned in to pick up Jackie in his arms. My mother shook me awake and I leaned against her as I sleepwalked beside her into the living room. My parents too, were very tired after the journey and left me to bring in the hand-made quilt that Aunt Hattie had given us. I curled up on the old couch where I fell again into dreamland. In the morning, I found a corner piece of the quilt covering me, and the rest of it on the floor.

Chapter 3

There is something to say about the familiar pattern to our life that held few surprises, but when they did come, it was with a jolt that made us appreciate the peaceful life we ordinarily led. It was not long after our trip that we celebrated the Fourth of July with a 'bang'. The employees of City of Wheeling brought the most spectacular fireworks to the top of our hill, called 'The Point' so that the citizens all around could see and enjoy the shooting stars and sparkles of colored displays that lit up the skies for miles around. The event would start in the early evening and go on for an hour or so. The sights and sounds of the fireworks brought out the neighbors from our valley and those from Elm Grove, a settlement located along the ridge at the top of our hill. It was the only time that my Dad did not call my brothers and I home with the sound of his trumpet. We climbed the hill as a family and enjoyed the spectacle first hand. When it was all over, we came back down to our valley, happy and excited with the noise and hoop de la that happened just once a year. It was on the fifth of July after the evening's entertainment, that my brothers and I went back up to the "Point", the place where I learned a valuable and painful lesson.

Lying all around us were the spent fuses that sparked the wonderful fireworks of the previous night. The other neighborhood kids were sitting on the ground with a rock in their hand, pounding the used contents of the fireworks that had not exploded. It would set off a loud noisy pop and thrill us a second time as we jumped back and laughed with glee. It was my first time to be so engaged. Tubby Namack showed me how to hold the package with one hand and pound it with the stone I held in my other hand. On the very first time that I raised my hand to set off the cracker, it exploded, tearing the flesh from the palm of my left hand. My brother, Billy, reached me as I set off a wailing that could be heard a mile away. He ripped off his shirt and wrapped it around my hand and we went home. When my mother heard what had happened, she called for my father to take me to the doctor. Thankfully, it was a Saturday and both my parents were home. Dad cleaned the grease off his hands that minutes ago were cleaning spark plugs. They rushed me into the hospital and within the hour, the doctor was sewing the pieces of flesh together. I don't remember if I was anesthetized or not, but I do remember how my mother was screaming at me for being so stupid, and my brother, Billy, stood by and cried. I was afraid to cry. I knew if I made one sound, my mother would swat me. Her mantra was that she didn't raise any dumb kids, and I didn't want to be the first one. Eventually, my wound healed and left a two-inch scar that ran from the exterior of my palm to the natural crease in my left hand.

The following week, the family again resumed the usual trip to one or the other of my grandparents. I showed off my bandages and gained much sympathy from my relatives and a pat on the back for being so brave and stoic when I got my hand stitched up. Most Sundays, we would gather around the kitchen table with Aunt Nora, Uncles Sam and Ralph, all children of the second marriage. I do remember the last I saw of my great Grandmother Hanke. It was in 1936 when I was ten years old that I was first allowed in the front parlor where my Grandmother was laid out in a casket. Lace curtains hung from the long glass windows in the rather small dim room, and mourners came and sat silently on the velvet settee for a while and we all just stared at the body of my oldest relative. After what seemed like a very long time, we came out to the kitchen and the lively conversation and much laughter began again. We never visited the house in Benwood after she died. My great Aunt Nora moved to Baltimore and I don't know what happened to the brothers. That is as much of a history of my mother's family that I know for sure, that they were Scotch, Irish and English and preferred drinking whiskey straight as they sat around the red-checkered oil-clothe covered table in Grandma's kitchen.

My father's people were German immigrants. I do remember my Grandmother Lautenschlager. Her hair was white and very thin. I could see her pink scalp underneath the wiry hair. She was very old and my mother disliked her and hated it when Dad brought her to our house.

Most of the time she lived with Aunt Lizzy and Uncle Isadore. They lived in a very nice home in Martin's Ferry, Ohio, which was always tidy. We occasionally went there for Sunday dinner, sitting very properly at a table covered with white linen and napkins, and a full service of china dishes and crystal glassware. Very little conversation went on during the meal served by a kitchen maid. My Mother seemed uncomfortable and said little as she adjusted our napkins and raised her eyebrows at my father indicating her displeasure at being here. We rarely stayed longer than a couple of hours.

I remember one Thanksgiving Day when we were invited to my father's relatives in Martin's Ferry. My mother displeased as usual about going, but deferring to my father's wishes, we crossed the bridge over the Ohio River on the way to Grandmother's house. Daddy had just paid the entrance toll and drove about fifty feet when he hit an icy place on the metal bridge. We whirled halfway around which put us in the lane heading back to Wheeling. When he turned the car toward the bridge again, the man in the tollbooth would not allow us to go on until Dad paid another dime for the crossing. Not even a persuasive explanation given by my father would move him, so he angrily turned the car around a second time and we went to Grandmother Hanke's house instead. I noticed the small smug look on my mother's face as she looked forward to a truly happy Thanksgiving, and picking up on the changed atmosphere, we began to sing "Over the Meadows and Through the Woods to Grandmother's house we go." Even my father seemed pleased and nothing more was said.

Chapter 4

I would wake up in the early days of autumn with the sound of the soft rain falling on the roof, and the howling winds whipping against the house with a vengeance announcing that winter was not far off. If an early cold spell brought snow, it came in gently, soft and wet. It might build up slowly, and then slide down the slanted roof with a loud thud. Ice cycles too, kerplopped when the sun came out, melting away the tenuous hold it had as it clung to the end of the rooftop. The dirt streets soon developed ruts from the tires of the few automobiles that came up through the hollow. We might see the last of the vegetable trucks that delivered the fresh produce from the farms, but the milk wagon continued throughout the winter if the snows were not too deep.

Winter was a very special time, and before you could get used to the rapidly changing fall colors of the trees, there came bare leaves and the stark naked loss as trees stood out against a bleak background showing the loss of dignity formerly exhibited by the lively growth that began in the spring. It didn't last long though, for soon the branches were lined with a light snowfall, almost like the cotton batting that filled the center of a quilt. The beauty of a first feather dusting of snow as it whirls around in a dance when the cold winds blow cannot be matched. It may be the first cold day before winter actually starts when the air circles around and does it's best to hold you back, and you wish you were still in the warm bed that held you fast just an hour ago. Even the struggle to be dressed in a new snow suit, bundled and buttoned up to a chin muffled by a scratchy wool scarf does not lessen the appreciation of what nature had wrought. The limbs of those recently full branches now hold the brilliant white snow, glistening with a hundred lights as the sun lightly touches down. I've seen Christmas cards that paint a similar scene, yet how could a replication match the experience of hot breath spewing out air that quickly turn to little clouds that drift away after you've spoken.

We had one sled between us kids, and it had one slat that lost its nail so that you had to hold it together with your body to kept it in place. My brothers put together a toboggan by fashioning two pieces of metal for the runners and a kind of inverted box to lie on as they took turns riding down the hill and making the dangerous turn around the S curve. Sometimes they made it and sometimes they ended up in the high drifts that were banked along the roadside. I usually made it to the S curve and pulled the sled uphill to beyond the Fisher place. On moonlit nights we would stay out until way past the usual time to go to bed. Our energy never slackened when there was fun to be had. When we finally gave up, it was because Mom hollered for us to come in.

When winter had made its way in and stayed long after the Christmas season had passed, my father continued to shovel his way out from the garage when he went to work. If the snow covered the walk, it too had to be shoveled to the sides until we could walk though a corridor of piles of snow on either side. Snowsuits were worn everyday, hooded headgear and mittens were used year after year. For whatever reason my mother had, the snowsuits she bought for me was always a forest green color. It took a long time for my mother to get me suited up, and before I knew it, I needed to go to the bathroom one more time before I left the house. I do remember one time after I had started school that the easiest thing to do was to just let go and suffer the consequences. Fortunately, it was on my way home.

Each year seemed different as far as the weather goes. Some years it snowed past March and into April, not snow that lasted but nevertheless, the sun could fool us into believing it was time to put away our woolens and get ready for spring. The hard rains and lightning streaking across the skies would be the start of frozen water holes that iced over and became a threat if you misread the hardness of the ice. Spring could be fickle. A bit of sunshine and warmer days could turn its back on you as quick as a rabbit tail could disappear down a hole. When I would shed my sweater or coat in that capricious weather, I would be sure to come down with a cold followed by a cough. Mom would rub goose grease on my chest and Vicks Vapor Rub on my throat and upper lip. The combination of the smell would knock over a horse. Sometimes it felt good to just lay in bed and miss a few days of school, if I was good enough to 'fake' a longer recovery period.

Every night, we sat in front of our Zenith radio and heard the announcer in a singsong voice, "Here we are at station W.W.VA in Wheeling West Virginia," the syllables drawn out in southern twang, "bringing you the country music of Gene Autry" (or some other cowboy singer of the day.)

The music played on the airwaves was typically cowboy and gospel songs. We had square dance music at the Hi-Up Club on the "Point" or down at beer joint down on 29th Street. Everything was western in those times. My brothers were given guns and holster belts for birthday gifts or Christmas presents and we went to cowboy flicks staring Roy Rogers and his partner, Gail. The Major Boze program brought a large number of contestants hoping to get a starring role in the field of entertainment. Saturday night listening brought us the sound of a squeaking door as the announcer introduced, "Inner Sanctum", with its spine chilling scenarios that took place in various cemeteries.

Another program was, "The Whistler" and his scintillating voice promising a thrilling evening. "I see many things as I walk by night" invited much and delivered little. Ghosts and ghouls filled the airways and our fears mounted. By the time we were sent to bed, we were afraid to climb to stairs to our rooms. Sometimes, my parents allowed me to bring my friend, Mary Kay for a sleepover. We learned to speak 'Pig Latin' quiet proficiently and confused my brothers to the point of 'mayhem'.

Chapter 5

It was 1934 when the Romanian Gypsies came up to our hill for the first time and stayed for a weeks. We curiously spied upon them as they pulled their colorful wagons into a circle just as the cowboys did, and set up camp in our neighborhood. In those days they still traveled around the east coast, stopping near large cities along the way to tour behind the carnivals that frequently came to town during the summer months. The gypsies camped near the well where fresh water streamed from the pipes drawing from the underground streams coming from the mountains.

I would watch them quietly standing behind a tree. I would peak out to see the dark skin and long curly hair on both men and women. All were dressed in colorful clothes. The women wore long full dresses and low-cut full-sleeved blouses, with necklaces and bracelets hanging from the neck and wrists. They scurried about, the men collecting branches and dried wood for a fire and the women cooked over the fire as it blazed into flames.

When they had eaten of the wild game or a stolen chicken or two from someone's back yard, the men would pull out cigarettes and the women would clean up the dinner mess. They laughed and talked and shouted in a strange language that I had never heard before. Guitars were brought out as the sun came down and the music from violins and guitars filled the night air. I watched, long after the sun had set and the shadows from the trees had disappeared and until a sound from my father's bugle startled me.

It was a call to come home and it broke the intensity of my fascination of the scene before me. I left as quietly as I came and walked toward the pathway that took me home. My mother warned my brothers and I about how the gypsies would come and steal white children and carry them off. Though my two brothers heeded the warning and stayed away from their camp, I stood behind the tree night after night as the gypsies ignored my presence and my hopes for an exciting life with this nomadic tribe was dashed.

School was usually over in early May and classes were lined up, some sitting some standing for a class photo on the porch of the 29th Street School. On the last day of school, report cards were passed out. I always agonized over my grades in Math. My other subjects were high enough to bring me up to a B plus, and the usual lower grade of C plus in arithmetic kept me on the borderline of an A. My brother Jack was held back a grade because he skipped school so many times over the year. He wasn't so much of a 'student', but he always managed to make his way through life with his likeable personality. He was working in downtown Wheeling when he was thirteen and somehow got hooked up with mob boss named, Bill Lias. What was so remarkable was that my brother was trusted by the biggest dealer in town; a man who owned everything between whorehouses, racetrack operations and slot machines. Jack's job was to collect the sacks of money from the slots and deliver the cash to Mr. Lias. My brother was about five foot eight at the time and with his innocent baby face, he could get away with murder. The following story was taken from the Wheeling Area Genealogical Society. I had always thought that maybe my brother had exaggerated the contact with Bill Lias but apparently he was giving the factual history of "Big" Bill as the that story pretty much agrees with my brother's memory of his time in the employ of one of the biggest mobsters around. Jack told me how he met Bill Lias. He was having a bowl of chili at a downtown café. A tough looking thug came up to him at the counter and the following conversation ensues.

"Hey kid! The big guy wants to talk to you."

"I don't know him," my brother said.

"If I were you, I'd talk to him."

"What does he want?"

"He wants to talk to you."

"Yeah. What about?"

99

The big guy had been listening to the conversation, and walks over to the counter and leans over my brother's shoulder.

"Hey Kid. Would you like a job?"

"Doing what?"

"Why are you asking?"

"I wanna know what kinda job?"

"Never mind, come and see me." He hesitated a minute.

"Where do you live?"

"In the Y.M.C.A."

"Do you wanna Job?"

"Doin' what?"

"Don't be a smart ass, if you wanna a job, come and see me at the club and ask for Bill Lias. My man here will tell you where to go."

The "job" turned out to be a carrier for money from the slot machines set up all over town; in clubs, whorehouses that Lias had an interest in and beer joints. When Jack got in touch with one of the men who worked for Lias, he was given the key to the slots and became a runner for the mob. When my brother told me the story as an adult, I looked Bill Lias up on the internet and found his story in the Wheeling Genealogical Society. Working with Lias after a few years begin to pose a threat to my brother. The man had taken a liking to Jack, bought him his first suit and pair of black polished leather shoes and a small Fedora. My brother began to emulate his walk and his talk out of the side of his mouth. Altogether taking on a gangster persona as Lias took him on the payroll like a son. One fateful night they were having dinner at one of his nightclubs. They had just begun to dig into the steak and potatoes when a couple of thugs came through the door with machine guns. Lias's men, always at the ready, spotted the two guys as they set off a volley of firepower toward the corner table. Bill pulled Jack by his coat sleeves and pushed his head under the tablecloth as he followed, his big frame caught the end of the cloth, pulling the mess of dishes filled with food and drinks upon the two of them. Bill pulled a gun from his holster and shot the two interlopers dead. Pretty soon, the dining room was filled with gunfire, patrons crawling across the floor to the exit doors and disappearing as fast as they could make a getaway. The next move was a bevy of cops entering the room with guns popping off toward the ceiling, and calling a halt to the medley of screaming patrons and gunfire. Lias turned to Jack. "Keep your mouth shut and stay covered. Don't move until I get things straightened out."

As soon as Bill crawled out from under the table, the cops were on him like fleas on a horse, pulling the nearly three hundred pound man to his feet, cuffing him behind his back. The cops had retrieved the gun that Bill had kicked over the floor to the table next to ours. Jack followed orders and stayed quiet until cops left and everything went still, then he crawled gingerly to the next table, lifted his head and saw only the cooks and waitresses over in a corner talking about what had happened. Doris, the woman who had waited on our table came over to Jack. "You better get lost, Kid, Don't come back here. Bill is gonna end up in jail on this one and you could be called as a witness. New get the hell outta here and don't show your face in Wheeling."

Well, this was the story of my brother's work with a widely known gangster who had operations from state of West Virginia, Pennsylvania, and Chicago, Illinois. It wasn't too long after his work with Lias that Jack joined the Navy at fifteen years of age. Dad must have manipulated the birth certificate so that he could enlist. He was discharged after WW11 ended. I missed my brother, but he was better off finishing his education in the Navy, rather than at the beck and call of a guy like Bill Lias.

Chapter 6

My mother's sister, Aunt Virginia, lived in California and when I was twelve years old she visited us for a month. When she was ready to go back to California, she asked my mother if I could come with her. My mother quickly acquiesced and we boarded the train in downtown Wheeling. My mother bought my first piece of luggage. It was leather and large enough to hold the few pieces of wardrobe decent enough to take to my new home in California. Aunt Ginny promised to take me shopping for a few outfits to start school in September. I was easily persuaded to join her on my first train ride that would take me through a dozen states to sunny California where I would spend the next seventy years.

The train stopped in Chicago. The city was larger than any I had seen. My Aunt and I had a three-hour layover there and I ate my first meal in a restaurant. We sat in booths and ordered from a menu with all sorts of food listed. Dad sometimes had taken us to eat sauerkraut and wienersnitzel in a German beer garden in Wheeling but we never experienced a real dining place like this. When we were finished, we walked the streets of the city. Streetcars and trains traversed streets filled with people. My eyes were drawn to the overhead bridges and tall buildings that lined either side of the streets.

It was late August when we arrived in Antioch, California and school would begin in early September. It was 1940 and after graduation, my brother Bill left to work at the naval base in Norfolk, Virginia. With a few years, my mother came west and my father sold our house on the hill and joined her in California. I look back on the wonderful years of my childhood, and truly in my memories, I am never separated from the hills I roamed as a young girl, a barefooted hillbilly from West Virginia.

THE CRAZY LADY WHO LIVES NEXT DOOR

MARTI AIELLO

Chapter 1

The last of the boxes were packed, the house was scrupulously cleaned or where paint was needed, that too had been done. She walked slowly up the stairs. She had done it so many times that she knew each step; twelve steps in all, and near the top she had put her hand to the railing to steady herself. At the landing she turned left and continued down the hall. There were smudge marks that once held the fingerprints of her children, now fully grown and in homes of their own. The newly painted bedrooms smelled of the odor that lingered. She had done the work herself and felt that a good cleaning of the dark hallway would pass inspection.

As Marne paused at the doorway of the room that she and her husband had occupied for thirty-three years, she hesitated a moment before entering. She had forgotten to empty the contents of the coal-burning pot-bellied stove. The ashes can stay, she thought. The ashes were what remained after everything was gone, her life, her belongings and the memories that had been so much a part of her after her husband died and her children had gone their own way. It seemed appropriate somehow. Her home at Riverview Drive was new . . . and different in every way from the two-storied tri-level house where she had lived.

"Marne," she heard Joe's voice, loud and impatient.

She went quickly to the window. "I'm just checking the rooms to see if I've forgotten anything. Be right there."

Marne felt a tad guilty that she had used her wiles to get Joe to help her with the move. Joe Ricardo had been a patron of the historical society where she worked and had shown an interest in starting a relationship. Her interest in Joe lay solely with a very large truck he used on his farm, and his muscular frame used to heavy labor. Joe revved up the engine of the truck and she hurriedly left the room.

105

Always the gentleman, Joe had stepped out of the truck as Marne exited the front door. He took her hand and helped her into the passenger seat, appreciating the view from the rear.

"How do you feel about moving into the mobile home park?"

"How do I feel? Umm. I don't know, maybe a little scared. I don't know whether I made the right choice or not. I've lived on this street for thirty-three years and raised four kids here. The house is too big for one person and the neighborhood had changed and it's time to move on. The Creekside Park is a senior complex so I'll be with the other OP's."

"And what is that?"

She laughed, "OP stands for old people."

"You're not old, honey. You're seasoned"

"Umm, I like that."

The trucked pulled away from the house as Marne looked over her shoulder, "Do you think a house has a soul, Joe?"

Joe raised his eyebrows, careful how he might answer her. He loved her, but thought she dwelled on things beyond his comprehension. He had married and divorced two times and it was always the same. Women think far too much on stupid ideas. His soul purpose was to get Marne in bed.

He had showered and shaved, put on a pair of jeans and a denim shirt that reflected his blue eyes. The sun had bronzed his skin and a shock of untamed hair held down with a cowboy hat gave him the appearance of a guy who had roped cattle and rode the range. It was an appealing look that had worked on most females, but not Marne. Her sole purpose for allowing the relationship to develop along for the last two months was to get her house in order and move to Creekside Park. When that was done, Joe would not get what he wanted, but Marne would. She wasn't a cold woman, just a practical one.

They had arrived at her newly constructed manufactured home. Joe left the drivers seat and went to stand beside the passenger side, extending his hand to Marne.

"Welcome to your new home, my lady."

As she held out her arms, Joe brought her up close to his chest. He hoped to try out the bed he had transported to the new home. As Marne left his arms, she felt for the keys to her new house in the bottom of her purse. Joe took it from her hand and opened the door, standing aside as she entered.

Boxes covered the floor of the living room. The furniture had been delivered and set up the day before. Joe took Marne into his arms again, aroused and waiting for the moment when he could get his reward. He had worked hard for this opportunity to consummate what he had hoped would be a long and lasting relationship with this woman he might even want to marry.

"I'm having my daughters over to see the house. I told them we would be here by two o'clock. Maybe we can get together next week for lunch at that place downtown, Joe. I want to thank you for all the help you have been during this move. Could I pay you for the work you've done? I appreciate all the time and effort you've put into emptying the garage and taking stuff to the dump. I don't know what I would've done without your help."

Marne moved toward the door that she had left ajar. She gave him a quick hug as in 'goodbye Joe, see ya around'. Confused as to what had just happened, he walked out and then turned around. "Can I see you after the girls leave?"

"I'll call you after I get things straightened out. Thanks again Joe." She closed the door and sighed deeply. "Well, that went well," she said aloud.

Marne looked for the box labeled 'bedroom' and rummaged around until she found the sheets. "White or mint green?" She found herself talking out loud lately. "Am I loosing it or what?" It had been over a period of years since her husband's death and recently she had dropped a number of activities that kept her engaged for a long time. Now with the move to a new neighborhood, she found expressing herself audibly more often than not. I must be getting old, she thought.

The girls did not come until later in the afternoon and by that time she had already shifted the boxes around the house and began to empty them one by one. It was nearly six o'clock when her youngest daughter, Francine, drove up to the house. She had brought her live-in boyfriend with her.

Marne hailed them from the backdoor as they drove in the space behind her car. At that moment, a woman appeared behind the screened-in porch in the house next door. She began to shout obscenities and Francine dropped her box from shaking hands as the woman continued with an onslaught of verbal abuse. Andrew and Fran just stood there with their mouths open in surprise at this woman's attack.

We gathered together as in defense from her filthy outpouring of unsuppressed rage. A neighbor on the right side of the house appeared at the window. With a questioning look of concern on her face, she had looked out then dropped the drape she had held in her hands as if to say 'I want no part of this.'

"Are you sure you want to live here, Mom?"

"I'll be okay Fran, don't worry about it."

Andrew had slid across the seat of his MG sports car. It was pretty obvious he wanted to get away, like right now, out of the neighborhood and out of town toward his nice safe apartment in Danville.

Fran gave him a glaring look, then turned to me and said, "Do you want me to stay for a while Mom?"

"No, honey, you go back with Andrew. I'll be okay. Don't worry now, I'll call you tomorrow."

"Promise me you'll call the police if she starts up again."

"I will Fran, don't worry now."

As I think back to that very first day and remember that this was only the beginning, I wondered if my life would ever be the same.

It was seven o'clock, the sun had set and it was starting to get dark outside. I went inside and closed the door, thinking that I'd better get an additional lock on the door, and wondering if this was an isolated outburst and perhaps the woman next door had misinterpreted some conduct on my part. I couldn't think of any thing, but you never know if she felt that I had snubbed her something.

I suddenly felt very tired. I had read my library book for an hour or so and began to calm down. I tucked the book under my arm and headed toward the bedroom. It was now dark outside and the streetlights had come on, creating elongated shadows across the way. The winds lent an eerie sound as it rustled through the trees. I turned the T.V. onto an innocuous program about the habitat of the desert fox and was lulled into a kind of stupor. The dim light of the clock had awakened me and I began to unbutton the blouse I had worn that day, turning off the television and the lights of the living room.

"What a day," I sighed as I walked down the long hallway toward the bedroom. I slipped out of my clothes and into a pair of pajamas. The soft pillow against my cheek comforted me as I succumbed to the humming sounds of the fan overhead as it went around and around.

A knock at the window of my bedroom caused me to bolt upright. I listened for a moment before I went to look out beyond the patio and into a darkened space that appeared to be figure that blended into the background of the bushes against the fence. I squinted as I searched and saw what looked like a women's body pressed into the brush. There was no movement and I thought perhaps it wasn't a figure at all but a bulge in the shrubbery. I stayed there, my spine tingling at the thought of a dangerous lunatic out there somewhere.

My usual composure and sense of internal strength had somehow shifted into a defenseless creature full of unnamed fears. My body had tensed and shriveled into a posture of weakness, and I loathed the feeling. I am safe in my own home now with locked doors that were between me, and the rest of the world. This was the thought that I clung to. I had lived alone for over thirty years.

"What is the matter with me?" I said the words aloud.

This was beginning to be a habit. Ever since I moved into this place, I began to feel nervous and uneasy. I had never before felt a sense of fear or anxiety that had lasted so long. What in god's name is this all about for Pete's sake?

I got up and went into the bathroom. Looking into the face of this old woman, hair almost completely white and eyes that were anxious and tired looking. I splashed cold water over my face and swiped it with a hand towel. "Okay, enough of this. Nobody can get in the house without a key. If I hear any other noise, I can call the police or scream my head off until a neighbor comes".

My words were reassuring and I lay down again, hoping to sleep until morning. And sleep, I did. When the pressure of a full bladder became too much to ignore any longer, I looked at the clock and jumped out of bed. I was ten thirty in the morning. I had slept through an appointment with my family doctor. I brushed my teeth and headed for the kitchen. The automatic coffee pot sent out a stream of hot air, as an intermittent red light signaled an absentminded owner.

I pulled my favorite cup from the shelf, filled it and walked outdoors toward the garden, feeling the first hint of fall weather in the last week of August. As I sat down on the outdoor swing that was aligned with the back wall of my bedroom, I saw the draped window next-door move ever so slightly as it settled into place. My thoughts went back to last night and the late night knock against my window.

When the second cup of coffee was finished, I heard the sound of the morning paper being slapped against the wall of the house. The sun was up and the day seemed to set the events of yesterday into perspective. I had just imagined the knock at the window and the figure in the shadows . . . I smiled at my own overworked imagination.

Chapter 2

There was so much to be done. The boxes in the kitchen had taken the entire morning to empty and still a few left to work on and perhaps finish up the next day. I did not step out onto the porch all that day, but continued to make a large dent in the process of unpacking. The music from a brand new radio/CD/tape deck sent my favorite melodies throughout the house. I felt so happy to be in a new neighborhood, setting down fresh memories and meeting new people of my own age.

School Street had changed. It no longer bristled with kids walking to and from school. A parking lot was built over the space that was once a playground. A primary, junior high and high schools were built and the streets became a noisy place to live. My oldest daughter urged me to move to a safe enclosed adult community on the other side of town.

My old house had only been on the market for a month when I had an offer that took care of the purchase of the new house, with funds left over for future leisure time to be spent on vacations. A call from my daughter with an invitation to dinner at her place at six o'clock was accepted with pleasure. I stretched my aching back and went back to putting the dishes in place in the cupboard. They would all probably be changed in some near future, but for now the boxes were quickly emptying of all the everyday dishes. The nice twelve-piece place setting of my good china was put on the higher shelves.

After four o'clock, I stopped work, showered and dressed for a night out. Ginni came over and we went out for dinner. We had a pleasant evening and finished with our meal around eight-thirty. She dropped me off and backed out of the driveway. I had forgotten to put the porch light on. I looked to the right of me at the open door in the house next to mine, dark and quiet, yet I was somewhat aware of a presence as I walked up the dark stairs to the back door of the

111

laundry room, fumbling for the key that I had taken from my purse. Just then the woman next door began a tirade against me, yelling incomprehensible sounds.

The only clear word I heard were shouted in a low guttural voice. "Get out of the sky!" she yelled. The onslaught was so sudden, so visceral, that I froze for a moment, dropping the keys that I had taken from my purse, hoping to get into the house and away from the sound of that woman who was obviously nuts.

I was shaking so badly that I could not function. I clumsily worked the door, punching the latch several times before I could push the lever in place and draw the safety chain across the doorframe. When I was satisfied the house was secure, I stepped into the dining room, my shadow visible in the frosted glass window that faced the crazy lady's windows. All the energy was drained away as I felt the power of evil embodied in this woman's tortured soul.

The hour was late and only the streetlight cast shadows of the trees that could be seen through the front windows, shimmering in the dim light of the moon. Unable to find the power to move, I felt glued to the floor as I continued to stare at nothing I could see, but only feeling the force of this encounter with a hellish power that had trapped me in its wake. I have no recollection of the time I stood there, but finally found my way to the bedroom where I laid down on top of the covers, weak and shivering with fear and cold in the last days of summer.

As sleep overtook my exhausted body, the earth had moved from darkness to light and I woke with the ordinary sounds outside of a truck moving through the neighborhood. The daytime ordinariness had calmed me to the degree that I felt my own power moving inside me again. As I lay abed, I planned what I could do to prevent this crazy woman from taking over my life again. I would go to the office of the manager of the park and tell her of the happenings of last night.

Chapter 3

My determination to put this weird experience behind me drew me out of the bed and stiffened my resolve to prevent any further harassment from the neighbor disturbing my peace. I was eager to try to put an end to this nonsense. I will go to the manager and tell her of last night's episode with the lady next door. Never again would I allow this woman to put me through another night like the last. After breakfast, I called the girls and told them what had happened.

Francine responded as I thought she would. "Mom, you should go straight to the manager and ask her to get rid of that woman. You have every right to live in peace and this woman has to go.

Ginny thought that I had over dramatized what had happened and I needed to get myself together and report the woman to the police if I thought she was dangerous.

When I went to the manager and told her what had happened, she advised me to go to Martinez and file a harassment claim. She also sheepishly reported that a few months ago, the crazy lady had been taken to "J" ward at Martinez because of her "problems". It seems that the woman had been diagnosed as a schizophrenic. Now what do I do? I thought. At the day's end, I felt very tired. I began to use the front entrance to avoid the woman. I left the house for any excuse that would cause me further anxiety. When I parked the car, I quietly closed the door and quickly came around to the front of the house and avoided turning on the lights.

My nights were restless and by morning, my body felt like I had no sleep at all. I continued to experience a weakness and a tired feeling that never left me. A doctor's examination revealed nothing at all. I couldn't tell him about the episode with the neighbor. It would sound ridiculous to attribute the condition of my mind to an incident that happened days ago. He would think that "I" was the one with the mental problem. And so I kept my thoughts to myself and suffered the 'aloneness' that seeps through the soul where others cannot enter.

Whenever I crossed in front of my window that faced the woman's house, I felt a wave of revulsion. She's put a 'hex' on me, I thought. It explained the fear and the feeling I had when I trespassed into 'her territory'. I remembered an old woman who had lived next to my home years ago when I lived in West Virginia. She would gather the children of the neighborhood together on the hot summer evenings when no one could sleep because of the heat, and tell us about the witches that she had seen and those who had she had helped to remove a hex that troubled the people who lived there.

It was all I could think of as I tried to go about my chores and shop for groceries. All of the ordinary things of life became too much for me. I was so tired all the time. I had begun to feel like I had lost my strength as I struggled to negotiate the four steps up to the landing, grasping the handrail and literally dragging myself up the stairs. My chest felt tight as I walked toward the bedroom. Not bothering with my clothes, I climbed into bed and lay quiet, panting.

My breath reduced to short intakes of air caused me to suck in what ever air that was left in the room. When I thought the atmosphere had expended itself, I stepped outside to breathe in the oxygen from the cool night.

She was there, the crazy lady sitting in the doorway to her home, sucking up all of the air, the rest of the world feeling the lack of one of the essentials of life.

I grabbed my keys, held my breath and ran toward the car, sliding across the seat as I attempted to insert the key. I pushed the drive stick and got the car in reverse and then gunned it out of the park where I lived. As I drove, not knowing where I was headed for, I literally felt a weight lift from my chest and my breathing had slowed down.

I used my cell phone to call my oldest daughter. The phone rang a number of times and at last she picked it up.

"Ginni, if you aren't in the middle of something, could I come and talk to you about a problem?"

"Sure Mom, Okay. I just finished with the dinner dishes and Jeff just left. Come on over."

"Thanks, I'm on my way." Ginny lived in Benicia and as I traveled toward the bridge that spanned the Carquinez Straits, I rehearsed what I might say. The scenario seemed straightforward enough when I thought it through, but it all sounded so crazy when put into words.

As I pulled the car to the curb near my daughter's house, I felt a bit sheepish as I knocked on the door.

She must have been on her way to the front of the house because she opened the door as I raised my hand to the knocker. "I hate to bother you with my problems, Ginny, but I don't know what to do."

"Tell me what's going on Mom. This isn't like you to get all stirred up about anything." She grabbed my hand and led me into the living room. "Sit down and tell me what this is all about."

"It's that woman next door to me. She's somehow put a hex on me."

"Oh come on Mom, get real. It sound's like you're the one with the problem."

"I know it sounds weird, but I don't know how else to explain it. I can feel evil emanating from her. She sits in the doorway without lights on in the evening, and if I go out with the car or come back, I feel this power she has over the whole neighborhood."

"Has anybody else complained about her?"

"Yes, the man and woman across the way have been to see Candy Richardson, the manager of the Park. When they first moved in this crazy lady did the same thing. You know, I don't ordinarily get upset about anything, but this is driving me nuts."

Marti Aiello

"Mom, I'm going to get in touch with my friend, Gloria. She works for a psychiatrist and I want you to go over and talk to him about this. He will be able to give you something to calm you down a bit. You can tell him the story you told me and maybe he can give some advice about what you can do to overcome this feeling. You know you are still going through menopause and maybe a little hormone can help you to feel normal.

"Well, thank you very much my dear and I'm sorry I bothered you tonight.'

I got up and left the house and as I drove my car out of the parking area, I nearly collided with some other driver as he drove toward the street corner. I could feel the blood beating in my ears and as I glanced in the rear view mirror, I noticed another familiar car had pulled out and was following me.

"My God!" I shouted this aloud, my voice echoing in the air around me.

When I came to the corner of the street, I turned right, then parked, pulled the keys out and ran to the door, pounding on it with my fists. Ginny had already turned off the living room lights and had been preparing for bed. She opened the door and drew inside.

"What happened? She asked.

"She's following me Ginny, the woman next door. When I got into the car, she was across the street. I recognized her. The streetlight was shining and she was looking at me. She started the car and followed me."

"Wait a minute, how could you tell it was her car?"

"It was the same license plate number, Y 1058416, I memorized it. Believe me, Ginny, it was her, Sheryl Newby."

"Look Mom, you've got to get a grip on yourself. Calm down and let's have a cup of tea. Do you want to stay here tonight?"

"No, I'll be alright. Maybe I over-reacted."

116

We sat quietly, both trying to sort out the pieces.

I took a deep breath as I felt my heart beating so hard my blouse palpated with each pulsating flow of blood. Ginny put her arm around me and I let loose with sobs that racked my body as she drew me toward the living room couch. When I had myself under some control and was able to breath normally again, I looked at my daughter's incredulous eyes. I don't think she believed me. I started to speak again but she interrupted me, looked at the clock and then sighed deeply, an obvious clue that indicated that she was loosing patience with me. I decided it was time to leave, no sympathy here. I'll have to deal with whatever comes. I struggled to find the keys at the bottom of my purse.

I pulled away from the curb, looking in every direction to see if I could spot her car. Nothing caught my attention until I got to the corner when I noticed the same black car. I sped away toward the bridge, hoping to lose her as I wove in and out of traffic, but she stayed tight against my rear bumper as horns blasted, trying to escape the speeding cars heading toward the Carquinez bridge.

I drove toward the bridge crossing, weaving in and out of traffic, trying to lose her, but she stayed tight against my rear bumper as horns blasted the ordinary sounds of street traffic. As I drove toward the crossing to the other side, I missed the turn off to East County and ended up on an unrecognizable Highway that gradually turned into a two-lane road empty of streetlights. I did not know where I was . . . lost on a dark road to nowhere with a maniac riding my tail.

"O God, what now?" I asked. She's going to finish me off and it will be a long time before anyone will find my body, I thought. The kids will be worried after a week or so and by that time I'd probably end up in an open grave somewhere.

The car began to hesitate and I looked at the gas gauge. "O God, I'm out of gas. Now what do I do?" I stared ahead and found a pullout with a forest of trees to the right of the street that sloped down toward a creek bed. I quickly pulled to the side of the road as the car behind me continued on. I turned my head toward her car and I could see that she had a look of surprise and consternation on her face. I got out of the car, running toward the bottom of the hill and then through the shallow stream of water to the other side. I continued up to the other side toward another clump of leafy green trees that were ahead as I continued to run as fast as I could until my chest was hurting with the effort.

I stumbled to a patch of dried grass and fell to my knees. There was no way I could go on. I listened intently as I lay there with my arms around my knees, curled up in a fetal position, protecting my body in such a way as to present the least amount of flesh exposed. I heard no other sounds except the dead quiet of a windless end of day, the clouds obstructing the last of the sun dropping out of view. My heart had stopped beating at a perilous pace and my body at last had ceased to tremble. The tension had relaxed and the muscles and tendons resumed its normal state.

My breath was now slow and quiet with each intake of the cooling air. It will be night soon, I thought. Now, what do I do? I don't know whether I can find my way back to the highway and try to get a ride home. The decision was not mine to make as my body relaxed and my thoughts soon drifted into a place of quietude.

The warm air was still and remained so until the morning sun brought a hushed rustle of forest creatures making their way toward the creek. Squirrels ran on a perpendicular trail to the tops of trees as small piece of bark dropped upon the dirty tear-streaked cheek of Marne Shaffer, "Orphan of the Storm".

*   *   *

Though the sounds were hushed as Marne's conscious mind began to shift with the clouded dreams that were receding into more distant past, her physical body felt the hard ground covered with the dried grass and the smell of forest reminded her of what was real and what was not. I wondered where I was and could I find my way back to the highway and be lucky enough to find an honest person to take me home?

Marne could hear the footsteps of someone or something approaching the safe haven where she had spent the night and she willed herself to be very quiet. A hand reached down and touched her cheek and quickly pulled away. Her eyes opened wide to take in a tall figure, poorly dressed in obvious cast-offs and holding a rifle by the handle with the business end pointed down; not at her but to the ground where she lay. Her eyes shifting wildly, frightened at his appearance, she tried to speak but her mind could not form the words that were needed to explain her presence here.

The man tried to speak but the vocal cords that produced speech had not been exercised in many years. Hoarse sounds finally began to make sense as he struggled to make her understand that he was not going to hurt her. Marne's attempt to articulate her presence here was almost as difficult.

These two psychically damaged individuals coming together in this place, what are the odds? What could she do? He seemed to want to help her, his eyes registered concern and he made no moves that would indicate that he meant to harm her.

The man leaned over, took Marne's arm and placed it around his neck when he noticed the dried blood from the scratches. Her leg was also scuffed up, especially the knees where she had fallen onto the ground. Her ankle had obvious signs of a sprained or possibly a fractured bone. He lifted her gently and tried to balance her evenly as he placed his feet apart to distribute the weight.

"Where are we going? I think I've broken my ankle."

"I have a place where I can take you, then we'll see about getting you to a doctor."

"Where is your house, is it nearby?"

"Not far, but it's not a house, just a rough cabin, one large room really, with a bed and hooks where I hang my clothes. But, it does have a nice old iron stove where I cook and a few pots and pans hanging on the wall. Best of all, a brick fireplace that spans almost the whole wall with a few hooks for my fishing poles and odds and ends of ropes. Like I said, nothing fancy."

The words he spoke were stilted and his voice rough as he stumbled through the explanation.

"I'm sorry about your wife and children. It is so difficult to lose people you love."

"What about you, what is your name?"

She hesitated, "My name is . . ." Her eyebrows came together, struggling to remember. "Oh yes, my name is Marne. Do you have any painkillers or even some aspirin? My ankle is really hurting bad."

"Hey, I'm really sorry, we're near the cabin now, I should have asked you if you were in pain. We'll be there in about five minutes and then I'll take care of your ankle and yes, I do have something for pain. Can I offer you something to eat? I try to get by with what I can grow or hunt so there isn't a lot of choice. Can you live with that?

"I'm sure I can. I've only eaten deer meat one time in my life, and I can't remember what it tasted like. I know it seemed different than the meat from my friendly neighborhood butcher."

"I don't suppose you'll be staying long. I need to ride into town for flour and sugar and some canned goods at the grocery store. I usually pick up my social security check from the post office once a month. Other than the basics, I can get by pretty well out here in the 'wild'. Speaking of food, I still have some of the stew left, I've got some homemade bread in the box and if you're on your best behavior, I'll open a jar of peaches." He looked at the woman he had found, hoping she wouldn't refuse his offer.

"How could I refuse, if you can put up with me a while longer, I'll ask you to take me back up the hill when you get my crutch made."

"Not a good idea, you wouldn't be able to make it unless we had a ski lift, which I don't, so you, my friend, must put up with this old man until we can get you to the point where you can walk. I'm sorry, but I couldn't carry you up the hill. "Do you have a car phone?"

"No." Marne made a face.

"I can go into town tomorrow."

"How do we do that, she asked.

"I have a horse. The woods are so dense here that you can't even get a land rover to blaze a trail through this area. Don't be worried about staying for a while until we can get you on your feet. I'm afraid you are stuck with me for the time being, so let's just take it one step at a time."

Marne's thoughts whirled around in her head. "You're right, I don't really have a choice do I?"

"I'm afraid not. I'm really glad this happened, not because you had a nasty fall, but that we met. I suppose I've just gotten used to being alone. It's been four years now. The time went by slowly at first and then I had a kind of schedule, hunting and fishing and working around the cabin, fixing it up so that the roof didn't leak, then I built the fireplace. I've mastered carpentry by building the shed for the horse, learning to ride comfortably. You should have seen me when I first started. My backside ached for a week. Then I build the cabin and most of the furnishings, bringing in the tools and cutting the trees for the lumber that I needed. It was an education, believe me."

"I'm impressed. Don't you get the least bit lonely?

"Sometimes I do. I might just kidnap you for a while. Would you mind?"

John's large grin crinkled his eyes as he caught the beginning of a concerned look that crossed her face. Marne wasn't quite sure if he were teasing.

"Are you serious?"

"Um, Yeah. I could be your nurse. After all, I am a lab technician. I could make sure we can wrap that ankle of yours with three-inch tape, prop you up for a few weeks while it heals and make a crutch for you to hobble around on. I'll go off to the store and bring back whatever your heart desires. How does that sound?"

"You are serious."

"Um hum" John's grin continue to spread, his teeth showing now. His eyes were dancing with the thought of having a woman around. Goodbye loneliness—hello happiness. It was a song he'd heard on his short-wave radio. It sort of fit the moment. The past few hours are the happiest he'd been in a long time. I'm gonna miss her, he thought.

"My kids are going to be worried about me, and I don't feel comfortable camping out with someone I just met. You've been a lifesaver, finding me, bringing me to your home and taking care of me, but I think I had better leave after you get this ankle wrapped. I'm so grateful that you happened to find me. I don't know how I could have managed with my ankle. I never could have made it back up the hill."

"Stay tonight at least Marne, rest up. It will be dark soon and there is no way you can manage to hobble up the trail to the highway. There isn't enough clearance or a flat place where we can get a helicopter to drop down and pick you up. I'm afraid you will have to stay here for a couple of weeks until you get on your feet." John had put out the facts and she realized the suggestion was one of necessity.

"All right, but just for the night. So where do I sleep?"

"In the bed, of course. I'll get my sleeping bag and rough it for the night. It'll be fine."

When he lowered the light in the lamp to just a flicker, the room darkened as he stripped down to his long sleeved underwear. It had been a long day and both John and Marne were tired from the tension of meeting the challenges of difficult maneuvering through the wooded hills to this safe and now warm cabin. The embers popped and sparked for another hour as the night darkened and sleep overtook the two strangers who had met only ten hours ago.

Chapter 4

John awoke first and put more logs on the glowing embers of last night's fire. He had already dressed and had his first cup of coffee and poured a cup for his visitor, hoping he could extend the time spent in the cabin a bit longer. The aroma had its effect and Marne stirred as the warmth of the kitchen and the smell of coffee drifted throughout the large room. She stretched and made moaning noises. Her ankle had swollen and the wrap needed to be loosened. She also needed to go to the bathroom. How embarrassing, she thought. No point in hiding the fact. She turned her head toward the fireplace. "Good morning, John. I'm afraid I will have to trouble you for my crutch and I need to use the 'Men's Room' if there is one."

"I'll bring you my bathrobe and some warm socks to wear. I could step outside until you finish dressing and then help you to the outhouse. That's the best I could offer at this point."

"It'll have to do for now."

"Your ankle is really swollen. Do your business and then I'll redress it for you."

After the toiletries and breakfast were taken care of, John made a list of supplies he had to bring back from the store. Marne was settled back in bed, her ankle rewrapped, with a pillow under her knees. John slipped on his wool jacket and, jingling the keys in his pocket, waved a good-bye and went toward the barn. The horse neighed and kicked against the backboard of the stall. After patting her down, he slipped on the halter, blanket and saddle. John put his boot in the stirrup and swung his one hundred and seventy pound frame onto the saddle. The trip into Martinez meant that he had to report the accident to the police and face the subsequent loneliness again. Maybe if I wait awhile, giving her a chance to heal, it might be that we can still have a relationship of sorts, he thought. Whatever

123

happens, it had been a perfect 24 hours, a time to think that perhaps my days of quiet could now be at an end. I think I could go back now and pick up my old life again.

He had reached the marker that proclaimed the town of Martinez, 3 miles. As the horse jogged along, the small company store near the shoreline of the Shell Refinery came in view. It was mostly canned goods and fresh meat that he purchased and paper products like bathroom tissue. It was a once a monthly ritual that had brought him in touch with humanity, but not to the point of conversation with anyone he knew. A newspaper headline caught his attention; black headlines proclaiming the murder of a woman killed by a black car that had been abandoned along the side of the highway. The owner of the car is believed to have forced the vehicle off onto the shoulder of the road, killing the driver and leaving her to bleed to death. The timing coincided with the day that he had found Marne. Was she the driver of the black car or the victim of a hit and run? John's mind began to rehearse the day that he had found her. She had been with him for nearly twenty-four hours yet she hadn't mentioned how she came to have fallen down the embankment or how she came to have injured her knee.

She indeed had revealed nothing about her life, the incident that had brought her into the wooded hills or anything else that would give him a clue as to why he had found her lying in the grass so far from home.

Curious, John began to look though the other newspapers for more details. He bought three, tucked them under his arm and finished his shopping. When he got to the parking lot, he stopped and shifted the heavy burden, then dropped the sacks under a shade tree before he sat down on an empty bench. One of the newspapers had a photo and a description of Marne Shaffer, forty-three years old and a resident of Pittsburg, a city just 15 minutes away.

As John began to read, there were more questions than answers. Why hadn't she told him where she lived, what was she doing running through the woods of Martinez where he had found her? What was he dealing with here?

The headlines read . . . WOMAN SUSPECTED OF MURDER . . . below the caption was the picture of Marne Shaffer with the following sub-text, "A murdered woman was dumped alongside a little-used highway west of interstate highway 80. Sheryl Newby, age 56 and a resident of Pittsburg, was found with her head bashed in and a bloodied rock lying next to the body." In a seemingly unrelated complaint detectives had been called to investigate a missing person, Marne Shaffer. Her daughter, Francine, had not seen her mother since moving her into an apartment in Pittsburg.

While the forensic lab was running fingerprints, including those of Shaffer, they discovered a match from the blood of Sheryl Newby that was left on the rock with those of Marne Shaffer. A black purse left at the scene of the attack was lying nearby with driver's license found in the wallet of Shaffer's purse. As the police were trying to piece together the evidence found at the scene of the murder, they uncovered the connection."

John Leighton's suntanned face had turned an ashen color as he tried to make sense of what he had just read. It can't be real. There has to be some kind of crazy, mixed up scenario that turned into a nightmare. The Marne that is lying in his bed back in the cabin can't be the same Marne that he just read about. Something is very wrong here, he thought.

The information in the newspaper disclosed telephone calls from the daughters of Shaffer describing some strange behavior exhibited by their mother just hours before to the two detectives that appeared at Ginni Shaffer's door. It appears that Marne Shaffer's neighbor, Sheryl Newby, had followed her from her home in Pittsburg to her daughter's home in Benicia. But, when detectives questioned Shaffer's neighbors at her home, they said that Newby's car had not left the driveway and that they had seen her sitting and smoking on her porch as she normally did in the early evening.

John read the other papers. No other information was found that would link the woman to murder. According to the report from the daughters, Marne Shaffer had claimed that Sheryl Newby had followed her all the way to Benecia. John had told her all of the details about the incident. Why had she not told him about the incident of her accident miles from her home in Pittsburg?

Puzzled, John's thoughts circled round and round in his head. He nudged the horse forward with a little more urgency than he usually did as he made his way through the dense trees to his home, troubled about what he might learn. He had envisioned a growing relationship between himself and Marne, maybe more than just an attraction. Now he was emotionally involved for the first time in years. He had felt a link between himself and this woman and a need to know her more intimately. John's life had turned a corner, he felt alive again. Last night had been electric. The warmth of Marne's body next to him had aroused feelings that he had not experienced in years. His throat became constricted with the anguish of something found and something lost. If only she had shared with him the story of how she came to be in the forest. What had happened before he found her curled up in the dry grass, injured and alone? All of the questions would have to be answered as he dug the tip of his boot in the horse's rib. Leaning forward, he urged the animal through the brush, thoughts filling his mind with questions neither asked nor answers given.

"What a fool I've been"! He said it aloud. Hoping that a woman I had met twenty-four hours ago, who literally dropped into my life out of nowhere, would be the answer to my dreams that had not even been expressed before yesterday. Now I don't even know if she is a murderer or if I'm being set up to provide her with an alibi. He felt sick in the pit of his stomach . . . So much for an interesting experience that gave him hope again.

Chapter 5

The daughters of Marne Shaffer had come together and sat sipping coffee at Francine's place in Walnut Creek. Andrew had washed dinner dishes and left the two women to talk while he moved on into the front room and was lightly snoring while the noise of the television droned on in the background.

"I don't know what Mom has got herself involved in, but there is no way she could have killed another human being. As soon as she is found, it will all be cleared up. The first thing a newspaper reporter does is to create an interesting headline. I swear if that reporter doesn't back off, I'm going to sue the son of a bitch." Fran's words had been spoken with a little too much volume and Andrew ambled into the kitchen.

"What's going on", he said.

"See for yourself. This was just delivered." Fran handed the newspaper off to Andrew.

"When did you see your mother last? Do you remember what she was telling us about the neighbor next door?"

"Sure, but that doesn't mean that she killed somebody. Get real Andrew, you know my mother better than to question her integrity. She's not a violent person."

"I didn't mean to imply she was. Your mother does seem to get herself involved in situations that are out of the ordinary. She did make a big thing out of the next-door neighbor. I think I heard the story about three times."

"Well, it was quite unusual for someone to make a statement like, 'Get out of the Sky', Fran retorted.

"Yeah, then she started to refer to her as "the crazy lady who lives next door. Maybe she started some 'bad karma' by referring to the woman like that."

"I don't know, maybe you're right. Lets not talk about it anymore Andrew. I'm worried about her not showing up. Wouldn't you be if was your mother?" With that she cut him off and turned toward her sister. What do you think Ginni.

"I don't know, Fran, I'm worried about her too. I haven't slept well since she left my house on Friday. It's Wednesday. The detectives haven't been any help at all, they just keep saying, "we're working on it." Then, we have newspaper reporters calling ten times a day to ask if Mom has contacted us. I don't know what to think. No matter what happened, if anyone can get herself out of a mess, Mom can."

At this moment in time, Ginni was right. Marne had not been able to process the situation; she had been running away from a mad woman who wanted to hurt her. Now she was being taken care of by a kindly man who helped her, bound her foot and made a makeshift crutch so that she was able to move around freely. The only disconcerting thing she felt was that her girls would be worried about her. But how could she call them? The man who had befriended her was disconnected from the outside world. The kids would be frantic and she had no way of reassuring them. John would be back from the store in a short while. As much as she was enjoying the friendship that was developing between them, she had to get into town and let the girls know that she was all right.

John had made up his mind. If Marne came clean about her relationship to the murdered woman, he would help her, shelter her, do whatever he could to bring her through this mess. He tried to sort out his feelings about what he would say when he confronted Marne with the information he had garnered from the newspapers. As he came nearer to the cabin, he saw the smoke drifting up from the chimney. A few more logs had been added to the fire and the smells of cooking permeated the air. He decided to wait until after dinner before bringing up the charges that were listed in the paper.

What a confusing mess. His head was aching and the prospects of bringing the whole thing out in the open had made him uneasy.

John had lost touch with humanity for such a long time that his time in a self-imposed solitary left him defenseless against the present entanglements that Marne was involved in. His head was aching and the mere prospect of bringing the whole mess into his previously simple life left him confused and disquieted. His manner was certainly not his usual one as he came down the last leg of his journey home. Heavy-hearted, he led the horse into the stall, latched the door and slung the satchel over his shoulder.

He felt an unfamiliar heaviness as if the newspapers had taken on weight. It was strange how his thoughts seemed cast darkness over the pathway leading into the house. It would never be the same, he thought.

Marne had found a large dishtowel made of an old flour sack and wrapped it around her waist. It covered the clothes she had worn every day since John had found her, now wrinkled and spotted with grim and grease. Under the circumstances, she could do no better. In the quiet of the evening, she heard his footsteps as he approached the house. He paused in the doorway, looking toward her with a questioning look in his eyes.

"What's up, mountain man, didn't your day go well?"

"Hardly, but I don't want to talk about it now. I see you've out-did yourself today. What smells so good?"

"Well, I found a stash of canned pasta sauce and I thought, with some spaghetti and mess of greens, we could go "Italiano".

"Sounds good to me. We need a little something to go along with the meal. I have a few bottles of merlot left in my make-shift cellar."

By time the meal was finished, the outdoors had become dark and the trees cast shadows along the rim of the property that had become a sanctuary for John Leighton for the last seven years. As the candles on the table had oozed wax down its slender frame, John's thoughts turned to the conversation he had dreaded to have that might destroy any future he had hoped to have with Marne. He finished the last of the meal and the wine bottle had been reduced to dregs. He pushed aside the plates, drew his fingers together and whatever had remained of the 'bonhomie' that he had clung to during the evening, was about to disappear like the melting candles.

"What is it John? You've been skirting around some kind of issue all evening. I'd rather you speak directly about what is bothering you. If you need to say something, please do it. I know we're just strangers thrown together by odd circumstances, but I'd rather you be honest enough to share what's on your mind than to keep it hidden and make us both uncomfortable."

"Give me a minute Marne, I've been in shock since I picked up some newspapers when I was in town and read about some awful thing that happened just before I found you in the woods. I don't know what went on before we met, but your picture and your life has been under scrutiny since a body was discovered near here".

John hesitated, trying to form his thoughts into words. "Marne, the police believe a woman was murdered and they suspect that it was done by you. What little I know of you just doesn't add up to you committing such a horrendous crime."

Marne's face had drained of all color. She looked down at her hands that were trembling as if apart from the rest of her body. "I don't know who could have done such an evil thing. But it wasn't me, or anyone I know. Who was it that was murdered? Is it someone I'm supposed to be acquainted with?"

"It was your next-door neighbor, Sheryl Newby. Do you know her?"

"Yes, I had a run-in with her when I first moved in. She was really weird, and as much as I regret it, I did say that I thought she was crazy because of her behavior the first day I came to live here. But I would never ever hurt anyone. You have to trust me. I'd never deliberately bring pain on another human being. I'm not that kind of woman. Please believe me!"

Marne had clasped her hands, her clenched fingers tightened until her knuckles were white and as her body shook with sobs, John drew her into his arms, muffling the sounds of her crying. He held her until the last of her sobs had become a chain of hiccups that eventually stopped.

"Marne, we need to go into the police department and report your accident. You need to explain how you had hurt your ankle and I found you and took you to my place to tend to your sprain. Tell the officers there as much as you can remember. They will probably try to agitate you and maybe even accuse you of hurting this Newby woman. Just try to remain as calm and detached as you can. The first thing the 'cops' do is to try to get you rattled so that you say something that could tie you into this woman's death.

"I haven't done anything wrong and there is no way I could have committed a murder. I've never even had a car accident before this. I'm sure that after I've told them my story, they can go after the real killer."

"Well, let's hope that is what happens when you see them. It's important that we do this as soon as possible. Are you up to going into the police station tomorrow?"

"Of course, we have to go now. As soon as we get into town, I need to call my girls and tell them where I am. They must be frantic over this if they've read the newspaper."

Ginny was on the telephone with the police ten times that day. What were they doing about this terrible thing? They were trying to tie her mother into this horrible situation that happened and they hadn't done anything except to tie her into a crime and raise a lot of questions that suggested that she was somehow involved in the Newby woman's death.

Chapter 6

Marne's fears were more than justified. John had brought Marne into the police department where she was given the opportunity to call her daughters. After the girls had vent their frustrations over the police interrogations, Ginni and Fran decided to contact a lawyer, one of the well-known legal representatives throughout the whole of Contra Costa County. His name was Nick Simmons. He had won a fair amount of fame for the work he had done for a well-known madam who shot a man who had molested a sixteen year-old prostitute. After the man had been serviced he had beat her so badly that three ribs had been broken and she had lost the sight in one eye. Her face had to be surgically restored. For this and other atrocities, the fellow was sent to prison for life, and Simmons had been in high demand in a large number of newsworthy cases.

It would be another twenty-four hours before Simmons was permitted to see his client. Detectives Farley and Kramer had more than sufficient opportunity to question both Ginni and Francine. Questions were loaded with a unique candor, seemingly innocent but enough to entrap the girls into becoming willing witnesses against their own mother without being aware of the manipulations of the two officers of the law.

In another set of unique circumstances, Marne's friend, Joe Mitchell, had picked up the morning newspaper and saw her picture and the headlines declaring her a person of interest in the case of the murdered man, John Leighton. Joe had not been able to let go of his desire for Marne. Even when Marne had brushed his feelings aside, he had hoped to be able to win her back. She had touched him where no other woman had. For a long period of time he sat at the kitchen table and read the tabloid through again and again. The cup of coffee at his elbow had become cold when he aroused himself and went into the bathroom to shower and shave.

After he had dressed, Joe went down the steps into the garage where he kept his vehicles. He hadn't driven his truck since he had helped Marne with the move into her house at Creekside Mobilhome Park. She had been part of his life for over eight months. He hadn't been able to forget her; each day whatever he did, however much he tried to put the past behind him, nothing worked. The sun came up in the morning and the evening sky darkened and he thought about Marne, always Marne.

The drive to Martinez took less than forty minutes. His heart beating to the sound of a rock that had embedded itself in the tires hitting against the road as he traveled at a steady pace toward the city where Marne waited in a cell. He had no idea whether he would be able to see her or not. But he would be there for her regardless of what had happened. The truck had lulled his senses since he left Pittsburg. His confidence had now settled in his psyche. Everything would be as it was when he courted her. It wasn't too late. They were meant to be together. He believed this with his whole heart.

Joe parked the truck, pulled out the toolbox that he normally carried and locked it up behind the passenger seat. He would need the room when he picked up Marne from prison. Joe picked up the pace as he ran up the steps of the courthouse. After he enquired at the front desk, he was given a pass and directed toward the temporary jail cells. The sound of the heels of his boot could be heard as he rapidly approached the room where he would be able to visit with Marne. She had been informed of his visit and was there, waiting. Her eyes searching his for some sign that she would be freed on bail. His smile promising that she would be able to walk out with him and go back to the safety of her home.

"Marne, I'm going to get you out of here. I've paid the bail money and you're coming home with me. Don't worry about a thing. I'm going to take care of everything. I know you can't be guilty of killing anyone."

Joe's reassurances and concern for her caused a flood of tears, her chest heaving with the release of emotions carefully controlled for too long.

Chapter 7

Detectives Ronald Farley and Alex Kramer were sitting at their computers typing up their reports of the accident that involved death of Sheryl Newby. Also under investigation was the incident involving Marne Shafer's convenient loss of memory about her own circumstance that brought her into the woods where Newby's body was found along with the fingerprints of Marne Shafer. Farley's opinion was that the two incidents were somehow connected. Kramer was more skeptical and felt the investigation had not gone far enough to have precluded other options.

Along with the witnesses conveniently related to Shafer, the other suspects and their testimony further muddied the water. Neither daughter could retract their original stories about their mothers' opinion of Sheryl Newby. Kramer pulled the old fashioned long-necked phone used in the nineteen thirty's toward the end of his desk. He leaned back in his large comfortable chair asked the operator to connect him to Marne Shafer. After three rings, Ms. Shafer herself picked up the telephone.

"Is this Mrs. Shafer?"

"Yes, it is. Who is this?"

"It's Alex Kramer. I would like to come over this afternoon. If you want to have your lawyer with you, that would be appropriate if he is available, I will also have a transcriber with me who will be able to tape the conversation. Do you understand?"

"Yes. I have no problem with that, but I won't be able to tell you any more about what happened than you already know."

"That is what I want to talk with you about. I simply want to verify your statements that were made when we last met. There is one other thing that I want to discus with you if you are up to it. I know this has been a trying time for you and we both want to be able to clear up this matter as quickly as we can."

"Yes, Detective Kramer, I will tell you all I remember, but so much is a blank to me that I'm not sure I can add anything to what we discussed before."

"Yes, alright Mrs. Shafer, I'll be over to see you within the hour."

Kramer heard no reply, so he carefully lowered the receiver to the cradle of the phone, took his foot off the desk and moved the comfortable chair forward as he bent over the chart with the name "Sheryl Newby" typed neatly on the tab. He scanned the pages of the brief and locked on the information already collected on the death and autopsy reports contained therein.

Something was missing that didn't quite add up. Who was John Leighton and how did he fit into the picture? A man who lives like a hermit meets up with a woman who is running away from something that she fears, ending up being cared for by this kindly gentleman in a cabin he had built in the deep woods. Kramer was not used to being faced with more questions than answers. All of these strangers came together in one big mystery that now needed to be unraveled, and nobody liked mysteries more than Alex Kramer. It was what made his pulse beat faster and stimulated his mind, as he would graft all the lists of probabilities and then mark the information on a chalkboard that would not be erased until his thirst was quenched and the mystery solved.

At the top of a large chalkboard that was the centerpiece of the room was the name of SHERYL NEWBY listed at the top and on a separate line, then below that, the names of Marne Shafer, John Leighton, Ginny and Francine Shafer. These were the major players connected to the murder of Sheryl Newby. Was Marne Shafer faking her amnesia? Did John Leighton know Sheryl Newby in a past life? Shafer's daughters seemed the least likely candidates for the murder since there would not be sufficient cause for them to want to eliminate their mother's next-door neighbor. There was always the possibility of another unknown person in this scenario, and so Alex Kramer put a large question mark next to the other names.

It was two-o'clock in the morning and Alex lay awake staring at the ceiling, counting the acoustical tiles across the fourteen-foot square room divided by a two by twenty-foot beam. The bed that he and his wife shared was king-sized, much too big now that she no longer lived with him. Alex was an excellent detective and a lousy husband. He knew it and his ex-wife sure as hell agreed with that assessment. In fact, so much so that twenty—three years of excuses for his absences at holidays or any other times you could mention, had added up to too many good reasons to not continue the charade of matrimony. The funny thing was that now holidays were usually spent together at either Alex Junior's place or his daughter, Gloria's house.

His wife had never re-married and he occasionally paid nocturnal visits that seem to satisfy both of them.

The four names hung in the air of the dark room with the mind of Alex Kramer focusing on each of them. How the murder of Sheryl Newby could be connected to the Shafer women or John Leighton just did not make sense. Leighton seemed to be a decent sort of fellow and the women didn't seem to have a good enough of reason for the murder of Sheryl Newby. Although the city of Martinez would need to stretch its budget a little thin, Alex Kramer would need the services of a psychiatrist who might be able to look a little deeper into the minds of Leighton and the Shafer's and perhaps determine which of the four may have a dark side capable of murder.

A well-known psychiatrist named Edmond Valkner was called in to assist the police. Valkner's reputation was known throughout the central valley area from Sacramento to San Francisco. He probed his victim's past, the suspected perpetrators and every other person connected with the case. It was Marne herself who provided the lead that brought in Joe Mitchell, the man who helped her move into the Mobil Home Park. His fate had nearly been bypassed until Marne has mentioned her friend who had been so concerned for her welfare when she was in prison. How he had visited her daily and paid the hefty fine when she was released on bail.

Valkner questioned Marne about her relationship with Mitchell. How seriously involved was she with this friend? She had responded to Valkner in an off-handed way that made him wonder how Mitchell felt about her. She was an attractive woman and no doubt could have a needy man do anything to hold her attention.

Joe Mitchell was added to the list of possible suspects and the Shafer girls were deleted from the chart that was the mark of Kramer's tools for dealing with his cases that received his careful scrutiny. The next morning following a night of pondering the likelihood of potential candidates for murder, Kramer's mind was fixated on Mitchell. As the light filtered through the curtains of his bedroom windows, he rose with a clear, unfettered mind. He dressed quickly, went into the kitchen and poured out a bowl of cold cereal while the coffee perked with a monotonous regularity until the scent of the brew could no longer be ignored.

Mitchell felt sure and confident that the case would soon be over and he could get back to his earlier routine, waiting for another interesting crime that would engage his complete attention and make his life peak again. He would never admit it, but he felt that he needed this kind of high to make himself whole again. He felt it in his gut. Joe Mitchell hung on the end of that question mark. He had known men like that before; so in love with a woman he was capable of doing anything to act the hero so that he could carry her off into his cave and live happily ever after.

The telephone in Joe Mitchell's house had rung at least ten times before he heard it. He was up in an apricot tree trimming the dead branches from the old tree that had seen many seasons and yet continued to produce fruit. He was happy these days. Marne Shafer would become his woman now. She clung to his arm whenever they went out in public. The time she had spent with John Leighton was beginning to fade along with the fear of being accused of the murder of the woman who lived next door to Marne. The house had been cleaned out and rented to an elderly couple that had lived simply and quietly with very few visits from their adult children. Marne had been able to increase her income significantly as Joe replaced the gardener and was very pleased with the arrangement. He had taken over the care of her fruit trees and the few shrubs that had been planted in the yard. Every thing seemed to be coming together for the couple and he had hoped to make it a permanent situation.

Joe dropped the trimmer into the leafy pool of debris that lay at the foot of the tree and moved slowly toward the ground. The telephone rang again and now he was near enough to the house to answer it. He went in and washed his hands in the kitchen sink. The ringing stopped and then another expected ring drew him into the living room.

"Hello, this is Joe Mitchell. Who is calling please?"

"This is Detective Alex Kramer and I have a few questions to ask you about the murder of Sheryl Newby. I'd like to have you come down to the station and clear up some details about the case that you might be able to help us with."

Joe dropped his head to his chest. "Why in the hell can't you just let us alone. We have cooperated with you on the case for seven months. My friend Marne is getting to the point where she is just putting all this behind her. Now you guys start the whole thing all over again."

"We haven't found the perp yet. When we do it's over. Until then, we need to clarify some points that puzzle me. And you sir are the only one who has something to gain in this whole scenario." Joe's breath caught in his throat and his began to stammer without any clear response coming through.

Kramer's eyes opened wide. We've got him! He's the one. Shit! I knew there was something fishy about this whole set up. He's on the line, wiggling like a snake. The guy is going to fry for this one.

Joe's eyes began to dance and his mouth took on the look of someone trapped in circumstance of his own doing; his lips thin and jaws locked tight. He began to clear his throat that seemed to choke on excess saliva. He couldn't speak for half a minute, not until he cleared his throat, trying to get control of his vocal cords.

Kramer left the line open while he connected with his partner, Jim Cannon. "Cannon, it's me. Get a car over to Marne Shafer's house and pick up her boyfriend, Joe Mitchell. I have him on the line, so do it now!"

Alex made his voice sound soft and soothing. "All right Mr. Mitchell, we are going to have to bring you down for a few questions. It's mostly routine, probably nothing to get upset about, just to clarify a few points as I said before."

Joe had the presence of mind to pull back and apologize. "Look man, this had been upsetting to Marne and I. I didn't mean to snap at you guys, but this stuff keeps coming up and we're getting tired of it."

Within seven minutes, Alex's partner was at the door. Jim Cannon had been on the force before Alex came on board. The stripes on his uniform spelled twenty years in service. He was a big man, six-foot five inches. His finely chiseled features belied his tough-as-nails determination to jail all the bad guys he could round up.

The doorbell startled Joe and his hands began to shake. His eyes shifted furiously as he realized he was caught in a trap that he might not be able to extricate himself from. For the first time in many years his confidence in his ability to use his plain old rancher persona had left him. He would have to open the door. Joe pulled his shoulders together and walked through the hallway and stood for a moment, arranging his face into a questioning expression that would be remembered by Officer Cannon. Joe Mitchell's hands were clenched into a tight fist to keep them from shaking and this fact was also remembered and belied his obvious attempt at being able to appear at ease.

"Good morning, I'm Jim Cannon, I've asked Alex Kramer to let you know I'd be coming to pick you up. If there is anyone you want to call before we go down to the station? I can wait outside."

"No, I can go with you now. Let's get it over with." Joe picked up his hat and pulled the door closed. The police cruiser with it's top red light flashing was noted by a few neighbors who had stopped mowing the lawn or washing the car and just stared at the policeman who was helping Joe Mitchell into the back seat of the waiting car.

All conversation had ceased and thoughts of what had been a relatively quiet and safe life before he got involved with Marne began to enter into his consciousness.

Chapter 8

Kramer and Farley sat in the office at station 41 in Martinez. Each of the men held the results of Edmond Valkner's assessments on Joe Mitchell in their hands. Jim Cannon was bent slightly forward, eyes staring off to the corner of the room.

"What do you think, guilty or not guilty? His eyes shifted back to Farley.

"What have you got?"

Farley hesitated before he spoke. "I think we can rule out the Shafer women, and I don't think John Leighton has the balls for murder. That leaves us with Mitchell, the guy who's hot for Marne Shafer."

"What about his alibi? Does it fit in with the time of the murder?"

"I'm working on it, Boss," Kramer shot back.

"Make sure you treat this guy with kid gloves. He is so nervous now we might run into trouble if we rush him into lawyering up."

"I'll treat him like a brother, Alex. I think I'll ask him to do lunch sometime this week."

"Don't be a smart ass or I'll send you over to work with Riley in the drunk tank."

Kramer laughed and scratched his backside before leaving the room.

Farley resumed his work at the old typewriter.

Chapter 9

Joe Mitchell was put into a cell with a man named Lawrence Richardson and another named "Schooner" O'Malley. Both men wore identical navy blue jumpers with a number on the right side pocket of the suit. Richardson nodded to Mitchell as he sat on the bottom tier of the twin bunks that lined the small cell.

"I'm Larry Richardson, and if I was you, I wouldn't lay claim to any of those bunks until your roommates get back. One is out for a piss and the other one is being interrogated."

"So, which one do I use", Joe replied.

"My top bunk is yours. What's your name?"

"Joe Mitchell, and I can't say I'm glad to meet you, but thanks for putting me straight, I don't want to get started off on the wrong foot. So Larry, what are you in for?"

"I killed two kids and left a mother pretty well smashed up. I was drunk and couldn't control the car. I guess I fell asleep at the wheel and rear-ended a woman driver with three kids in the back. They weren't wearing seat belts and when I hit the car, they flew across the front seat and two of the kids were killed and the other one is in the hospital with multiple fractures. The mother of the kids is still in a coma. My guess is that I'm going to do jail for a long time. The lawyer I hired is trying to get me into the Livermore prison if I'm lucky. From then on my trial will probably take some time, 'til then my life belongs to the state."

"Hey, that's tough, man. For your sake, I hope you can get a quick trial and get this behind you"

"Yeah, well thanks and same for you, man." With that said, Richardson leaned back on his bunk bed and picked up a book he had been reading.

Joe climbed up to the top bunk and hung his legs over the side, waiting for the other two men to make an appearance. It didn't take long before the other prisoner, Walter Hung, came back from the bathroom. He looked wild-eyed and confused. He began to talk in Chinese. The attendant guard pulled him inside the 10x10 cell and pointed to the bunk that he was to occupy. Hung bowed and quickly took a seat on the lower bunk. The fourth member of the cell made his appearance soon after the Chinese man had been seated. "Schooner" O'Malley, a redheaded Irishman with a three-day beard entered the room and looked around to check out his cellmates.

"Well, I see we have a new-comer to our little group. Now let me guess, you don't look like a drunk or a child molester, looking toward Richardson, so I'd guess you might be the one who killed the lady from Martinez. Am I right matey?"

"I didn't kill anybody, buster, so shut up until you know what you're talking about." Joe had clenched his fists, his eyes had narrowed and his full lips had thinned as he addressed O'Malley.

"Okay, okay, no big deal. You try to start something and we can duke it out when I get outta here. I sure as hell don't want to spend another day with you gents, so shut the hell up or I might change my mind." O'Malley slammed his big frame down onto the thin mattress. The metal bunk beds shuttered and moved an inch toward the metal rungs of the cell. The uniformed guard stuck his head in the door.

"What's going on here?"

"Nothing." Richardson called out. "Everything's cool, man."

The relationship between the two men began an endless two-week period when neither backed off and finally, Joe Mitchell, was spending his time with his lawyer in preparation for his trial. O'Malley was released and Joe moved to the prison at Livermore.

After a lengthy trial, Joe Mitchell was sentenced to life at San Quentin. Marne and her daughters, Francine and Ginny, had become witnesses against Mitchell. Each day was another bit of time to build on the original attraction between Marne and John Leighton that had brought them together. Just one month from the day that Joe Mitchell was sentenced to life in prison, Marne and John were married.

Chapter 10

THE HILLBILLY

Or "things my mother never told me about the birds, the bees and other surprising parts of life that happened when I grew up".

I was born in West, by god, Virginia and was by virtue of geography, a "Hillbilly", but by virtue of femaleness, not a 'Billy' at all.

The adjective, "ignorant" added to hillbilly is an appendage that explains much and was well deserved.

My summer-wear was overalls or shorts (without a top) and bare feet that were free to roam the hills whenever the spirit moved me.

When we kids were bad and my mother was mad, she called my brothers and me . . . "you little heathens", as in, "Git in the house this very minute or I'm going to give you what for". I guess when we were playing Cowboys and Indians all feathered and painted up, my Mother must have believed we were really Indian children.

We had a front porch with a swing hung from the rafters, and one evening when I was eleven, Mom was singin' and I was swingin' when she noticed a swelling on my chest around my "dimple". She said, "honey, looks like you been stung by a bee right there." It didn't hurt so I let it pass. In a few weeks though the other "dimple" started to swell. Now I had two of them critters attack my body and they left a permanent protrusion that had to be tamed with my little brother's diaper and pins, and I couldn't go outside without a shirt. On top of all that, the winter I turned twelve years old, I woke up with dirty brown stains on my underwear. When I told Mom she said it was "the curse" and I might expect it to happen again. Now, the only thing I knew about curses was it had something to do with magic words, which didn't sound too bad. She gave me some torn sheets, folded like a pad, and she made a belt to go around my waist, and more of my baby brother's diaper pins. She told me not to kiss and boys, and she let me stay home from school that day.

There was a lot of things my mother told me, like "stop picking your nose", and "wash your hands" and "take a bath" and "when you git older, you'll learn a lot more. And I did.

CHILDHOOD MEMORIES

Transplanted from the green hills of West Virginia with my mind and heart as free to roam as the place I had lived, now a new home where grownup's ruled and children were schooled—to obey while in their presence. I was expected to be a 'lady'.

Growing Up . . . untamed mind and a with a spirit freed from mundane things as thoughts formed to draw my own conclusions of this new world.

The freedom of boys who could fish with their fathers and hang out around the wharf had more appeal to me than being a girl, indentured with small siblings hung on unformed hips. Or hanging wet clothes on lines stretched from house to fence pole.

I DIDN'T KNOW HOW TO BE A GIRL

I could climb trees and explore caves and pick blackberries; but this new status of femininity scared me. I was absolutely, positively certain, I'd probably gum it up!

MARRIED, WITH KIDS

I never got a chance to be a "Hippy" and wear flowered dresses that touched my ankles or Birkenstock sandals and to wear a wreath of flowers around my hair. I never smoked pot or got high with a guy on a summer day in the woods. I never carried a peace sign in a parade with a mob excited about civil rights, gay rights, women's rights or the right to die or marry same-sex partners.

I never went away with a guy in a band or lived in a commune with people who hug trees and chant mantras, devotees of the newest earthbound "holy man". Tempting as it was, I never traveled on the back of a "hog", hanging onto a tattooed man in black leather breeches. Rock bands came and stayed on and I didn't go to Woodstock or even the Fillmore to watch the performers who encouraged silly women to throw hotel keys and underpants at them. I never saw a male stripper and certainly would not temped to part with a buck to decorate his G-string. The only dirty four-letter word I knew did not start with and "F". But darn it, I do like to have a little fun now and then and be frivolous in my dotage. It isn't only fair, since I was such a model citizen who followed most of the rules and gave birth to children who turned out to be of the conservative persuasion (and never did jail time) that I could be a little outrageous and wear a Japanese kimono when I make a meal of tempura for a Sunday meal?

You would think that my kids would be a little more appreciative of my efforts to enhance the presentation of a lovingly prepared dinner with at least a small round of applause . . . but no, not on your "tin type". The eldest just looked at me when my sleeve dragged a little through the sherry and shoyu sauce and asked if I might be more comfortable in a change of clothes. Hells Bells, now that I'm through with raising these educated well-bred kids, I need a break. I want to sew some 'wild oats, buy some tap shoes and learn to dance like Fred Astair before I get too old.

THE HILLBILLY

Chapter 1

As was common in he early 19th century, the countries in Eastern Europe began to colonize the east coast of America. By droves, the Scotch, Irish, and English boarded ships to America to settle in the provinces of Virginia. As a child, I recall a trip up the mountains of Virginia to visit the place of my Great Grandmother's birth. My father at the wheel of an old Ford V8, traveled up the mountain to a log cabin in the woods. The house was built on the side of the hill. It had a dirt floor and a ladder leading up to a loft where we slept on mattresses made of chicken feathers. A large open fireplace on the first floor was made of rock and cement and was kept burning all day. A large metal soup or stew pot continued bubbling over a low heat and kept the house warm.

My great grandmother "rubbed snuff", and the crease at her mouth, brown with the juice of the tobacco staining her lips. Her cheeks were wrinkled and her hair was plaited and wrapped around her head twice. I never saw her without a faded cotton print dress and black cotton stockings held up by twisting the top and knotting it under. She wore ankle length paten-leather shoes with laces crisscrossing and then tied at the top. Her hands were gnarled with blue veins snaking their way down to the fingers. Her nails were kept short and her ring finger held a thin gold band that still shone in the light despite the fifty years or so.

There was an outhouse located a few yards down from the house. Ceramic pots were placed alongside of the beds and were emptied every morning. Quilts of used clothing provided the bedding used to keep the family warm. Rifles were hung above the fireplace, and used to provide the family with deer, rabbit or squirrel. A wooden barrel was always filled with water from a river, just below the house. Fish could be caught in the streams that led down into a river. Every thing needed was naturally provided for the families that lived in these early times.

The members of a family were expected to pull their weight. Children were a utility. Young children took care of younger children. All Mothers at that time breast-fed babies and many were taken by illnesses in their early years. As a girl reached past puberty, they married and reproduced. As the years passed, many of the people on the "Hill" left their homes and the life they had lived and moved to the towns and cities that were springing up in the South. As my great, great grandparents died off, the life they had lived disappeared, and a new life began as the younger members of the family left the hills and moved to the cities of West Virginia.

Wheeling, a city of about hundred thousand was an industrial town and the smoke from factories such as the home of U. S. Steel consumed the lives of the workingman who fed the open hearth and shoveled in the coal that was the very blood of the industry. The whole city had a pale of smoke that hung over the homes that were built to house the hundreds of workers, clad in blue cotton shirts and work stained pants. My uncles, Ralph, Chester and Jim worked there as did most of the men living in the area.

Grandma Hanke had passed away and her body laid in a casket in the "sitting room". It was the first dead person that I had seen and I was allowed to go into the front room that overlooked the railroad tracks that ran parallel to the Ohio River. The drapes were drawn and a candle at the head of the casket flickered across the face of my grandmother. The flame jiggled a bit whenever the train passed, causing the features to move slightly giving the illusion of the old woman's flaccid cheeks quivering with remorse for her death.

Meanwhile, my grandfather sat with his pipe in hand by the round iron stove in the small room between the kitchen and the sitting room. The odor of the tobacco and the smell of death created a sober moment until I entered the kitchen. My uncles sat around the big round kitchen table that held small whiskey glasses and bottles of liquor. My mother and aunts were sharing stories and laughing with high squeals of delight as they relived moments of their life together under grandma Hanke's care. My grandfather, father to my mother and aunt Virginia and great aunt Nora, had grown up as sisters. Aunt Virginia had already moved to California in 1926, the year of my birth.

* * *

She climbed up the hill from the "Hallow" where houses dotted the landscape below. It was her favored place to hide from her mother's view. And to lay upon the soft green spot barren of trees where she could look at clouds; puffy white clouds that moved and beckoned her into an internal dialogue with God. She had tried to hide her ignorance of this mysterious being that she learned of from listening to the Sunday school teacher, and from the other kids who had allowed her to tag along to a church that she had begun to attend. Her mind took her to the first time she had followed her friends, Margaret and Buddy, to the big brick building that could be seen below and over the other side of the hill she had climbed.

The spirals of the Catholic Church could be seen above the treetops as she made her way down through the rutted trail that still held a bit of water from the last rainfall. When she had finally arrived, she stamped off the dirt from the muddied shoes she wore. She quietly moved to the far side of the church and slid silently into the shiny walnut pew. She could see the magnificent painting of saints kneeling at the foot of an elevated Jesus surrounded by angels. Old women with black shawls wrapped around heads and shoulders knelt on the hardwood kneelers, heads bowed and rosaries in hand silently murmuring repetitious prayers. She mimicked the old women who sat next to her, moving her lips and wishing she had some beads to hold. She felt so out of place, and wondering whether if she would be asked to leave because she did not have a hat or scarf to hide under.

A bell rung and everyone rose from their seats and kneelers to stand. She saw a flag in the corner and brought her hand to her forehead to salute the flag like they did in school. Her face reddened and she trembled when she noticed that she alone had made such a gesture. An old gray haired women who had sat next to her, gently pulled her hand down and shook her head. It seemed that she was learning all kinds of new things about her world that was foreign to her. She had overheard a tale from Grandma Hanke that might explain why she had never been sent to church. One of her mother's Cousins had been sent to a catholic boarding school to be educated. And while she was there a discovery was made regarding the discovery of the remains of newborn infants stashed away in vault. The news was broadcast far and wide across the nation. The investigation of this horrendous find caused such an uproar that the school was closed down and the ramifications caused hundreds of catholic to turn away from the church.

The incident was not forgotten by my family, and those left behind would suffer the consequences. The results of this terrible tragedy and the resulting estrangement was that my brothers and myself would not receive communion and the blessings of the church until we grew up and married.

My father had served eight years in the army during WW1 and four years in the navy. When he had met my mother, Rosella. She was living with my great grandmother. Her mother had deserted her and my aunt Virginia after a short marriage to my great grandfather. "Jock" McClelland had also served in the Scottish Navy and met my great grandmother Mary Margaret McCleod of Edinborough, Scotland. Her mother, Sarah Virginia Lancaster, was born in England, and had seven children, Edward, Luther, Elizabeth, Rosella, Molly, Clark and Gladys.

My grandfather was William Fredrick Lautenschlager. He was born in Germany and came to America in the early 1880's and settled in Ohio. They became dairy farmers. My great grandmother was born in Belair, Ohio and her name was Daley. They came from Ireland and homesteaded land and became farmers.

The beauty of the hills and mountains would never be forgotten. I felt like I had an insight into my past. These sturdy pioneers had passed along in their genes, not just strength but also the ability to not only to survive but also to prosper in ways that did not require money or manufactured goods. Very few immigrants came from Europe with money to invest in property. Most were hard working, simple folk whose ingenuity and a strong back built houses, dug wells for water, started productive gardens and developed the property they owned and lived a good life. Children were used to help out and had a purpose in life. Work and play were part and parcel of every day activities. By the time a child reached ten or twelve years old, they were introduced to work habits that lasted a lifetime.

I would ask for no other life. A healthy mind and body and inner spirituality have been my rock all these years and I wouldn't change a thing as I go into the twilight years of my life.

Lost in Pompeii

A TRIP TO ITALY

Our flight from San Francisco was an agonizing nine hours of sitting in a three-seat, cramped space with barely room for our legs bent inward. It was merely the introduction to a trip I had looked forward to for months; a trip to Italy with a number of old-family Italians, some descendants from Isola Del Femmine who had been from pioneer families who came here in the early 1900's. Some I had known, or knew of by reputation. Many were first generation families who had literally established dynasties: direct descendants from the first builders of a small town along the rivers of the San Joaquin and Sacramento rivers.

Commercial fishing and canning had employed the majority of Italians who had immigrated here between 1900 and 1920's to Pittsburg, California. It was a small town where everyone knew his neighbor and shared a single heritage, coming from the small town of Isola Della Femmine to exploit the natural resources of the rivers that flowed toward the San Francisco bay.

After our airplane had landed, my adventures had begun. Our first days in the capital city of Rome, was an enjoyable cultural event, seeing the Vatican and touring the art galleries. I had been in Italy many years ago and briefly visited the area with a Polish woman and her brother who had shared my home when she moved to America. She had traveled extensively and we had stayed nunneries throughout the tour.

This trip was different, for I had traveled with many of the third or fourth generation Italians, many who did not speak the language of their grandparents, but who had visited Italy several times over the years. We spent two days, on a tour of the Vatican, than boarded a train to Florence to see a plethora of beautiful pieces of famous

153

art pieces. On our way south, we stayed at Hotel Eufemia, owned by a mother and son who felt it was the woman's personal duty to converse with the Americans in a loud, shrill voice in the Italian language, directing us to the dining room by vigorous nods of her head. She was rude and dismissive but friendly enough to those who spoke Italian. Most of the people that I traveled with spoke or understood the language and were descended from families of the original settlers. I had much to learn as we traveled along European highways and met many of natives who were very happy to share the history and glory of Europe.

Italian TV has a copycat "Dancing with the Stars" as a popular talent show but of a rather lower caliber. Young girls are shown doing the "pole dance", scantily clad, overly made up with heavy eye shadow and accented dark eyes. I don't know whether this kind of clothing which didn't leave much to the imagination started in the US or in Europe, but they certainly out-do the American performers by a long measure. I was shocked by the differences between the Italians that I lived amongst and the young people of Italy with today's mores. The young women of Italy led the world in fashion and the rest of the Europe and America followed.

I had much to tell my family when I returned home. The Italians that I knew, and after marriage to an immigrant family from Sicily, I was told much of the heritage of those who left Italy in the early 1900's and about the early days. Time had stood still for them their mores and values of those times had been inculcated into their lives and were far removed from the people of the culture of today. I can only write of my own experiences when I visited Rome. I can only say, I was caught up in the history of the times and experienced many wonders to say the least. I will tell the story as I lived it.

Our group from California had landed in Rome and was rested enough to go to the "jewel of the city, The Vatican". The finest artwork in all of Europe was on display and hours of enjoying the original masterpieces of art was a treat for us who had eagerly looked forward to our visit. The day was warm and pleasant, and the curators of the museum were more than delighted to point out the original artwork and period furnishings. Moving on, most of people that I had traveled with followed one of the curators while I continued to spend time with a most interesting gentleman who had joined our group earlier. Obviously knowledgeable about the artifacts, I was captivated with amount of knowledge he shared with me.

We were more than rewarded for our efforts. After a short rest, we were on our way south to Florence and then on to my first visit to the ruins of Pompeii. A group of us had walked up the cobbled streets toward the mount of Vesuvius. The history of Pompeii as told by our guide reminded me the fall of many nations whose pride, ambition, schemes and careless use of slaves and underlings used to serve the rich eventually are themselves destroyed.

Memories of much of the trip to Italy, fades into the background of my mind as I write of my unique adventures in one of the old ruins that many have visited over the years. It was the third day of our trip, and we had scheduled a trip to Pompeii, an ancient site of what once was a monumental engineering fete upon which the Roman Empire was built. Just a few walls around the temple remain of what was the finest piece of work by master craftsmen that could be offered to the gods. Creative genius was used to build an aqueduct bringing fresh water to the city where thousands of people lived and prospered. Valuable water that was coaxed from the Mount of Vesuvius kept the city of Rome abundantly supplied.

Greek slaves served the Romans, debauchery of a kind that chilled the heart of only a few that had not fallen into the trap of the rich and powerful was the normal for all. The Holiness of God had deserted those who had grasped fruits of the land and disregarded the poor and lowly. The gods they worshiped was power and might. The Roman navy had ruled the waters and judiciously directed the sluices so that the rich were served and the others, numbering into to he hundred thousands were left without.

Slaves were put death for venial sins. The accidental dropping of a plate could send a slave into the fishponds to feed the ells. In time, though, the gods would exact vengeance.

It matters not what monuments were built to the gods, the builder of waterways that served the city to ease of living for the rich was not the god believed to be sequestered within the mountain of Vesuvius. These gods would have their revenge upon those who stood upon the backs of the poor. As long as the centurions, dressed in full regalia and carrying his spear as a weapon to be used generously upon the backs of lesser men, now ruled the city. The rain could fall upon rich or poor and bless them equally for quenching their thirst. But that was not to be in a land where water was limited and the mountains source gingerly guarded by Aquarius. Not a god, but a mere man that judiciously guards a limited amount of water released by the mountain.

The history of the beginning of Rome was fascinating and the story was narrated by a very interesting man who spoke proper English and kept our together for a short time before they moved on to the next exhibits. I had been so caught up in listening to the story of that time that I did not notice that the group I had been traveling with had moved on. My eyes searched over groups that had formed around a speaker, but I didn't recognize any of them. I began feel panic as I went from street to street. Each place held a number of white tents that sold anything from books to trinkets of all sorts. All of them looked the same.

It was about three o'clock in the afternoon after hours of searching and I became disoriented and felt faint. And back to the ruins of the city that we had visited earlier, up the cobble steps I climbed one more time toward the western slope. A luminous cloud had appeared over Pompeii, and the scent of smoke and a corona of fire above Vesuvius filled the air. For a period of time I stood there, bewildered by what my eyes beheld. Everyone had left the area and I stood alone, confused by what I could not understand. A veil of white engulfed me and I felt disembodied, utterly alone buried in the ash of the fire that had long ago destroyed the ancient city's walls and roofs. A burst of fire from Vesuvius now and then erupted within the site of the dense buildings that leaned and toppled just a stone's throw away from where I stood.

My head was filled with frenzied thought of dying here in this country where no one knew of me and could not even identify my remains were I to be consumed by the fire that raged before my very eyes. I needed to lie down and rest before I go on. A stall of sorts could be seen a short distance from where I stood and I made my way toward it. It was a small enclosure surrounded by the same sort of tent material that covered most of the structures where I had found myself just minutes ago. But now the space no longer held knick-knacks but was filled with barrels of grain and livestock. Goats and live foul in crates set up a cackling and bleating that added to the noise of horses neighing off in the distance. My mind drifted off into another time, another place.

My body, curiously numb had succumbed to sounds of the tumbling of rocks hitting the ground just meters away. I woke and felt the ash of burnt pumice covering my nostrils so that every breath blew away the dust that covered my face and body. As I raised myself, I heard the rustle of stones falling from my chest onto the dirt ground as it settled around me. The volcanic ash of Mount Vesuvius had been carried through the air as the wind from the mountains blew over the area.

I tried to lift my right arm and found that it was buried under a foot of sand, stones and ash. My left arm lying across my chest had less dirt and I could move it slowly to the surface. I arched my back and the debris that covered my body shifted to the ground. I stretched and raised my self so that I was free from the encumbrances of the soil and ash.

I heard a strange voice calling out.

"Claudia, Claudia. Wake up. Are you all right? You must have fainted from the heat of the eruption of Vesuvius. We have seen the smoke coming from that direction. The city is now in its path and most of the servants were sent to find you. Many of the temples have collapsed, and the Gods have deserted us. The people are swarming into the streets and raiding our houses as they stand empty."

"My name is not Claudia, my name is Beatrice. Who are you?"

"I am your sister. Why do you jest at a time like this?"

"I don't know you. I have no sister. Please help me to find my friends."

"No, Claudia, come with me and do not talk in riddles at a time like this. Many of the servants have deserted us. Only Meletis and Casius have stayed with us. You must come now. The whole city is being deserted. I waited for you and when you did not come I brought Meletis with me, but we became separated when the walls of the city began to fall."

157

"Please help me. I don't remember anything before I found myself in a small stall when I woke. I just know that I am not supposed to be here, but I don't know where I belong."

Beatrice shook her head, impatient now with her sister, her head filled with the scenes of destruction that now lay before them. She thought her sister had injured her head and became confused.

She stood with are arms encircling and protecting the girl, eyes now filled with tears. "Everything is gone now, Claudia. The Mount of Vesuvius has tried to swallow us up in his belly. Come with me now, back to the house of my father and we can find food and a mat to rest upon. Perhaps my servants have stayed close and they can provide us with something to eat.

The woman who called herself Claudia hesitated a moment before speaking, then whispered to me in a quiet voice, "You mustn't bother father with your silly chatter, your mind is playing tricks on you and we must find a way out of here." I closed my eyes, willing myself back in time before I climbed out of the ash and found myself in the hands of this woman who rescued me from the street.

"You must remember me Claudia, I am your sister, Beatrice. Everything is gone now. The Mount of Vesuvius has tried to swallow us up in his belly. I will take you to our father. Don't talk nonsense in front of the servants. He will become upset with both of us."

The woman called Beatrice, and who called herself her "sister", held me closer, encircling me, then drawing me into her arms.

As the two women walked through the ancient city, courtyards could be seen as chariots came though the gated enclosures, revealing frescoes adorning the walls of the homes of wealthy Romans. An opening in the roof of the houses allowed a rainfall to fill a pool with fresh water. Claudia caught a glimpse of servants carrying water in artistically fashioned pitchers of bathtub of bronze metal, as a girl in a flowing white toga stood by impatiently tapping her sandaled shoe as she waited for her bath. The two women undressed and once bathed, slipped on the white togas that the servants had provided.

"We must go now Claudia, father is waiting for us and we mustn't worry him. You know how he is, he will be furious and have the servants whipped because they ran away and left us."

I could only remain quiet, for whatever I saw was like a dream to me from which I could not escape.

The mountains belched and rumbled one more time. Beatrice looked closely at her sister's head wound and finished her ministrations. Her arms wrapped around her 'sister', she led her on toward the main house where she was brought before her father.

The kindly face of the man, Claudius, for whom his daughter was named, stood before the women, his eyes inquiring why the two girls had allowed the servants to abandon them. He placed his hand over his heart, his face anguished with fear for the safety of his daughters and his wife. "We must go now, the servants have fled and we are in danger. Bring your cloaks and all that is precious to you. Everyone has fled and the mountains threatened to send an avalanche of molten lava. We must go quickly."

The courtyard was filled with people hoping to flee not only from the danger of the flow of lava, but the hoards of human beings screaming and running toward the river that had been the beginning of the viaduct that would provide water for the people of the region. The waters would cool them from the heat that had begun to affect them all.

They stood near a roman column, and as the old man grasped Claudia, pulling her against him more roughly than he intended, her head smashed against the wall and she fainted at his feet. Claudius bent toward his daughter, tears gathered at the corner of his eyes.

"My dear one," he whispered, "What have I done to you?" He looked toward the man who carried the spear. "You . . . help my daughters", he ordered.

"I am Attilius sir, I am the Lord Giaus' servant. What happened here?"

"And I am Claudius who gave the orders to bring back my daughters, and who are you to question your Lord?"

The man fell to the floor, prostate before his master. The spear that he had held was now in the hands of another servant.

"Throw him in the Dungeon," 'Claudius shouted aloud, though there was no one to hear . . . all had fled the courtyard.

"Mount Vesuvius has erupted and we are lost. The gods have deserted our people, and now we stand before the mighty hands of the god of the mountains."

"Nay, my Lord, replied Attililus, we will pray to the God I serve. He is Lord of all and he will protect all who ask of him. Bring your daughters to me."

Claudius picked up his daughter Beatrice, lifting the most precious gift of his life. Her very breath had left her as he laid his ear against her chest. "She is dead." He gently put her into the arms of young Attilius, trusting to the god he served. "She is in the hands of your god now. Show me the power you boast of."

Attilius bowed his head. "Lord God almighty, if it is your will, bring life to this beloved woman." The movement of her lashes, then the eyes that stared intently at this young man she had never seen, but somehow trusted, caused a tear to wet her cheek. Claudius moved toward Attilius and lifted her slight body into his arms and wept. His beloved daughter was now alive and well.

Now, the noise of workers filled the air. The backs of men, bent from the waist, black from the constant sun of Africa, broke the lumps of hardened rock along the roadway. The sweat from the effort of hard and tedious work trickled down cheeks of the slaves that felt the sting of a whip from overseers demanding more of them. One man, a tall light-colored African beat on a drum of sealskin, creating sound that echoed through the narrow streets of Pompeii. Twenty pair of eyes searched the faces of white men with knotted whips, ready to slash the backs of hoards of creatures brought from Africa to serve the white men. The stink of these strange men added to the dense smoke from the not too distant Mount of Vesuvius.

"Let the slaves go", Claudius shouted.

Tension filled the air. Not only in the minds of the slaves, but of my own heart . . . not knowing how I came to be in this place filled with fear and the power of men paid to drive other men to build roads for horse and chariots.

The woman who had called me Claudia, tugged at my hand, urging me forward to an enclosed compound, toward a half-opened gate guarded by a Centurion who grasped a spear in his right hand.

"My Lady bids you and my Lady Claudia, to go to him in his chambers. There is unrest and many of the servants have left."

"First, I must take Lady Claudia to the baths and let her change her clothes. Please inform my father of this, Baccus."

"Yes, Lady Beatrice, I will do so, many of the Ladies of the Court have gone back to their families and only a few servants remain."

The two women held hands as they walked toward open marble halls where the baths were located.

The woman called Beatrice, and who called me "sister", held me closer as her arms encircled mine. A high-stepping white horse had been brought by a servant and was now in the hands of Attilius.

"I will ride ahead and tell your father the news that you have been found and are safe. Do not veer far from the road. There is a pool ahead and you might rest there awhile."

As we walked through the ancient city, courtyards were exposed as chariots came through the gated enclosures revealing frescoes adorning the walls of the homes of wealthy Romans. An opening in the roof of the houses allowed a rainfall to fill a pool with fresh water. Claudia caught a glimpse of servants carrying water in artistically fashioned pitchers of bathwater to a bathtub of bronze metal as a girl in flowing white toga stood by impatiently tapping her sandaled shoe as she waited for her bath.

"We must go now Claudia, father is impatient for us to go quickly and we mustn't worry him. You know how he is, he will be furious and have the servants whipped because they ran away and left us".

Attitilius rode ahead to the palace of Claudius to inform him that his daughter had been found and were now at the pool of Mountain waters of Vesuvius. But Claudius was furious at the news that his daughters were so close and was left alone with none but the gods to watch over them.

Attilius, worn out with anxiety of his responsibility to find and deliver Beatrice and Claudia, had done his duty. He had brought the women back to the city safe and sound. His Lord and master was now shouting with disapproval of his actions when he had merely followed their orders to allow them to bathe in the mineral waters.

"My Lord, they insisted on going to the pool, what could I do?"

"And I am Claudius who gave you orders to find them and bring them to me, and now you question your Lord?"

Attilius fell to the floor, prostate before his master. The spear that he had held as high servant was now in the hands of another.

"Throw him in the dungeon", he shouted aloud, though there was no one to hear . . . all had fled the courtyard as the angry mountain rumbled and let loose a torrent of loose stone and fire.

The noise of the world around me roused me and I heard the sound of what I perceived as Italian speaking foreigners. The scenes of the past and the rumble of the mountain had subsided. I found myself lying on a grassy knoll. Beyond me were the canvass tents that had held the trinkets where crowds of people gathered. I tried without success to communicate to disinterested visitors or venders who turned their back to me as I tried to explain that I was lost. I had never felt so helpless in all of my adult life.

I was tired and disheartened as the hours went by and my efforts to communicate went unanswered. I began to look at everyone who passed me by and used the Italian word, "poliezia, with a questioning look and most just turned away, not wanting to bother. My impression of the Italian was not what I had expected. They seemed cold and uncaring and finally, as the day began to end, I found a kind English-speaking middle-aged man who took me to his car and drove me to the police station where I found Jimmy Cognilia, our guide, inquiring for me. I felt so utterly grateful that I choked on the tears that I had kept under control for so many hours. My, and others prayers had been answered and I safe, and somewhat embarrassed for the trouble and anxiety I had caused others.

I was once again among friends. I never told anyone of the strange encounter with history in the time of the total destruction of the city of Pompeii. Who would believe it?

The Cat

Sofia and Zoe were bored. They were visiting me from their home in Hawaii. A third granddaughter who lived in Guerneville was also visiting. Three little girls were sitting on the couch wriggling around, each attempting to occupy the four-foot space, did not bode well for the start of our vacation time together.

"What do you want to do today?" I asked as I looked over the morning paper. My eyes had turned to the photo of Sylvester, the cat.

"Do you want to go by the animal shelter?"

"Yes, Yes" they shouted, before I could finish the sentence.

"Get your shoes on then, and let's go." The girls scattered, looking for sandals and tennies that had ended up under the couch and behind chairs. My granddaughters, Sofia, Zoey, and Freddi had been visiting me during the summer and now were filled with anticipation about the trip to the shelter and we wasted no time as they grabbed their shoes and raced to the car.

I had thought about getting a cat for sometime now. Dogs needed to be walked, and I had observed the residents of this senior complex, where I resided, walking through the neighborhood with terriers and other small dogs. This scene did not quite fit my idea of leisure time retirement. Caring for a dog meant walking on rainy days in the late fall and winter and the hot, humid days of summer. Neither did the idea of watching gold fish swimming in a glass bowl appeal to me. The clubhouse had a large aquarium and I might peek at the fish and turtles once and that would be enough for me.

The animal shelter was just a few miles away and as I drove toward the town east of my house, it gave me time to rethink the whole idea.

"Remember, girls, this visit does not mean that we will make up our minds right away, so don't set your hearts on bringing a pet home today."

In ten minutes we were at the shelter. We parked and went through the double doors of the large brick building. A receptionist was plunking away at the computer.

"Could I help you?" she asked.

"Yes, I would like to take my granddaughters through the shelter."

"Just go through the hall to your right."

I could hear the dogs barking as we opened the door. An aide was grooming a large Great Dane. There were a number of cages that held all sorts of dogs, some barking at the interruption, others lazily glancing up as we made our way into the maze of holding compartments. Cats were beyond the first group of animals and were housed in a separate area in the back of the building. A shorthaired cat with tuxedo-like markings pushed out her right paw toward me. I had laid my hand on the wooden shelf where the cages rested. She appeared mild and unaffected by our presence. Her forepaw connected with my hand and her yellow eyes, dilated and questioning, drew me closer. She laid there, her body fully extended, forepaw covering mine . . . and I was in love.

Except for an uneven white streak that ran from the forehead to the black-tipped nose and an area of the chin, she was black, though her underbelly and forepaws were snow-white. Her eyes never left mine and neither did she lift her paw from my hand.

Sofia, Zoey and Freddi had watched the interaction between the cat and me. "She wants you to take her home, Grandma." The little girls searched my eyes, pleading silently and I could not disappoint them. I went toward the front office and stood in line to make the arrangements to adopt the first cat I have had since I had moved from my old house to the senior complex where I now live. She did not make a sound as she was transferred to a small cage, looking over her shoulder at three happy girls and me.

We brought Cat home. I opened the latch and she came out, stretched and walked like a queen back to the bedroom and lay down at the foot of the bed. I cautioned the girls not to follow her, but allow her be comfortable with her new surroundings. After the girls were picked up a few hours later, Cat and I spent time on the sofa, exchanging friendly information about each other. (Actually, I read a dossier about her background.) She was brought to the shelter when the family she lived with had young children who mistreated her, and the parents decided that she needed to be placed in a quieter environment. I, on the other hand, felt like an animal might be just what I needed, and my granddaughters needed something to make their stay more interesting. The time that we have spent together had been good for both of us. Our days and nights have been interesting. I usually turn in by ten o'clock or so. Cat sits on the glass table and looks out of the window. It's our time when I've read until I begin to nod over a book I've been reading, or fall sleep through the last part of a T.V. serial. We look at one another and agree that it's time to turn in.

It is usually around six o'clock when I wake up. She, Cat, walks across my prostrate belly once or twice and we get up and begin our morning: me with a cup of coffee and Cat with a bowl of milk. We have been together for three years now, both of us considerate of one another's foibles. She's never grumpy or out of sorts, and I don't need to get dressed if I don't want to. I can walk around in my pajamas and read six chapters of a book without a disgruntled comment. She loves me even when I talk on the phone for an hour. I never hear a complaint about food that is overcooked or undercooked or served too often. She's cool with everything I do.

Although Cat is mostly indoors, I allow her time for her meandering through the garden. She sometimes curls herself up, then will stretch out and lay between the chrysanthemums and the other bushes and flowers as I pull weeds and uninvited grasses.

Living alone is sometimes a bore. Cat livens things up a bit as she races down the hallway of inlaid wood flooring, slipping and sliding as she reaches the back bedroom and jumps from floor to bed with a repeat performance back to the kitchen. If I've left nothing in her food dish, she will let me know by a smart "meow", her tail erect as she struts toward the hallway and into the bathroom where I keep her food. I follow her, and she looks over her shoulder to see if I got the message.

It isn't always a non-verbal communication between us. I often talk with her and she nods her head or purrs in commiseration of complaints from me of missed telephone calls that I couldn't get to in time. 'Why do callers hang up right before I pick the phone up?" Cat agrees with a scornful look at the telephone. "I can't find my shoes anywhere" as I find myself on my hands and knees, looking under the bed. Cat will join me and she will look around the room until our search ends and I remember that I had left them in the living room.

My best companion ever will stay by my side until the last page is turned in the book I'm reading or the television signal ends the night's viewing. "Time for bed", I say. Cat agrees its time and heads toward our room. She waits in the bathroom as I brush my teeth and change into pajamas. It is after we have slept our eight hours and the sun comes through the window to awaken her, then she stretches then walks back and forth across my chest. I keep my eyes closed, pretending that the lump sitting on my tummy will get bored. She doesn't. I carefully open my eyes carefully and she stares at me for a time. I keep on pretending sleep, but she doesn't buy it. I have become her morning chore that she performs until I get up to greet the day. It is 6:30 and it usually takes me a few minuets to make it to my feet. She waits patiently until I pull on my robe and head toward the bathroom. While I sit on the stool, piddling away, she jumps up on the sink and I run the cold water for her morning libations. She only drinks water out of the spigot.

I go into the kitchen and put on the coffee and a bit of oatmeal for breakfast.

Cat waits at the counter for me to join her for breakfast. Actually, she has already nibbled away at her Science Diet Cat Food. At one time I tried a cheaper brand, but she would have none of it. The neighbor's cat was not as picky as my little girl.

The sound of the newspaper hitting the floor of my sun porch causes Cat to look out of the glass door in the front of my home. It is now close to seven o'clock. She turns her head back to tell me to fetch the paper from the porch. It is then that we start our morning with a cup of coffee and some communal time on the couch reading the news of the day. Content to sit by my side or sometimes between my out stretched arms as I hold the paper, the next thirty minutes or so sets the pattern for the day. On warm summer mornings she likes to jump from our porch, and crouch down between the bushes and quietly begin to stalk a butterfly as it bathes in the sun.

Kitty-corner from my house, a neighbor adopted a mottled brown cat that loves to strut across the street and visit the house next door. Deliberately turning around to observe Cat as she guards my house, her demeanor speaks volumes as she teases her adversary.

We've had our adventures too. One night Cat was sitting on the table near a window that looks out over tall trees that line the back of my neighbor's house. I woke up to the sounds of Cat hissing and scratching at the screened-in window. I looked closely at what appeared to be a bushy-tailed fox attempting to attack my cat as she sat on the table near the window. Its nose was pressed against the screen of the open window. I jumped from my bed to the side of the table and quickly closed the window. My heart was racing as I thanked the gods that be for saving my best friend's life. I sometimes think of the end of my days here on earth and hope that she will be here as long as I am. We have become best friends, someone to talk to, care for and share my life with.

Wintertime is warmer as Cat lays at the bottom of my bed, keeping my feet warm. She has certainly gone beyond all the rules that I had originally set and in the early morning, I sometimes wake to this creature that has now become my bed-partner, taking liberties, which were certainly not in our original contract.

Her meals are taken in the bathroom, where she had not yet learned the skills of toiletry. Included in my housekeeping chores, is the clean-up time. She is quite fastidious and does not tolerate a dirty litter-box. I sometimes feel that she takes advantage of my good nature. If I have spent too much time away from the house, she will growl when I come in the back door. Of course, much of the time, she is napping. Her full-body stretch is pure poetry in motion as her body elongates to a full three feet. The soft white underbelly invites a belly rub, which is given with pleasure.

When I perform my morning oblations, she is there at my side. Somehow she has made it easier to live alone. Cat joins me at the breakfast bar, quietly sitting alongside as I partake of my meals. There is never a cross word between us as we enjoy each new day. There are times when I must go off to a meeting, and as I start the motor of the car, Cat will haughtily walk toward the lawn swing or sit on the wall that divides the property line next door. There are times when my day has been too long, I will get the "cold shoulder", and she does not respond to my call. When she is over her pouting time, she will let me know. It is difficult to be without her and I worry that she has disappeared. She is part of my life, and I am part of hers.

We all need somebody to lean on and Cat is my best friend.

The Great Spider Hunt . . . Occasionally an insect might get into the house, be it fly, or another creepy crawler, and her wild animal instinct kicks into gear. Her body goes into a crouch; yellow eyes maintain a single-minded stare on her prey. Slowly, she inches closer to the object of her desire. Her hips are raised and her tummy almost touches the floor as she gathers the dust from my hardwood floor. Closer and closer she comes, her ears twitching with the anticipation she feels as the bug is within her grasp. Suddenly she pounces. "Gottcha", she purrs, her eyes widened until almost nothing is seen except the black center of the iris. He tongue flipping in and out of her mouth, her black paw holds the frightened creature to the floor nearly squashing it, but not quite. A live bit of food is essential to her animal nature. "Science Diet" is fine, as it goes, but there is nothing like the taste of a live, struggling morsel to add to the ordinary meals served by 'yours truly'.

Much of Cats days are spent outdoor on the porch. The connecting panel of glass doors is where she sits and observes with her eyes on the world as she observes the neighbor's cat strutting up the street as if she alone was Queen of the block where we live.

Well, I got news for her. IT'S MY CAT WHO RULES HERE!

POETRY

BY

MARTI AIELLO

Autumn

LEAVES FALLING

ONE

ONE

BROWN AND CRUNCHY UNDERFOOT;

SOME, CLINGING TO FAMILIAR BRANCHES

ARFRAID TO LET GO

UNTIL A GUSTY WIND BRUTALLY WHIPS IT OFF AND DROPS IT.

A DRY AND DUSTY TORN THING DRIFTS SLOWLY TO EARTH

STILL HOPING FOR THE BREEZE TO CARRY IT

JUST A LITTLE WHILE LONGER

BEFORE IT LOSES THE BATTLE AND CAN NO LONGER DANCE.

ARBUTUS, ARBUTUS;

YOUR SMOOTH REDDISH-BROWN SKIN, PEELING IN THIN STRIPS REVEAL

NOTHING OF SIGNIFICANCE.

YOUR CAPE OF LEATHERY, LONG LEAVES, SO SHINY

ON TOP, WITH THE

CONTRASTING DULL GREY LINING LEAVE ME BREATHLESS.

SMALL ANIMALS FIND SHELTER AS, THEY CLING TO YOUR STRONG, STRAIGHT YOUNG BODY

I ENVY THE AIR-BOURN CREATURES THAT SWOOP DOWN INTO YOUR BRANCHES

AS YOU HOLD THE CLUSTERS OF BRILLIANT RED AND ORANGE

BERRIES WITH YOUR FINGER TIPS.

YOU PLAYFULLY SHIMMER AND SHAKE WITH EVERY BREEZE, TEASING BIRDY TASTE BUDS.

The Memoirs of Miss Demeanor

Confessions of A Latter Day Saint

IN MEADOWS GREEN, A MUSTERING
VICTORIAN GENTS LAY LUSTING
WHILE CORSETS CAME UNBUSTING
AND NEVERMORE SO TRUSTING
WERE THE LADIES OF DAFFADIL HILL.
FOR THE GENTLEMEN QUICKLY RECANTED
OF THE LIES THAT WERE TOLD WHILE THEY PANTED
AND FATHERS AND BROTHERS JUST RANTED
ABOUT THE GREAT COST, OF INNOCENSE LOST
IN THE MEADOWS OF DAFFADIL HILL.
THESE LADS NEVER KNEW WHAT THEY STARTRED
WITH THE LADIES WHO WERE SO OPENHEARTED
THEY WOUND UP IN COURTS, THESE ELEGANT SPORTS
AND NEVER AGAIN CAVORTED
IN THE MEADOWS OF DAFFADIL HILL.

Weather Forecast

CHANCE OF RAIN, CLEARING BY EARLY MORNING

YOU HAVE THIS CLOUDY DISPOSITION
THAT POURS RAIN DOWN ON ME.
WHY CAN'T YOU JUST SHIP OUT ON THE RIVER
OF TEARS I'VE SHED OVER YOU.
THE SUN WILL COME UP IN THE MORNING
LIKE IT'S BEEN DOING EVER SINCE I CAN REMEMBER
WHY CAN'T I PIN MY HOPES ON SUCH CERTAINTIES AS THAT.
NOT ON SUCH TRIVIAL MATTERS LIKE WHETHER YOU LOVE ME OR
NOT.

I do alright alone, and better together,
       But . . . I do very poorly when semi—together
       In solitude, I do much
       In love, I do more
But in doubt, I only transfer pain to paper in gigantic passion play,
complete with miracles and martyrs and crucifixions and resurrections.

       Come to stay or stay away. This series of passions poems
are becoming a heavy cross to bear.

THE FINGERS OF MY MIND REACH OUT TO TOUCH YOU
THRU THE HEAVY FLOW OF TALK THAT THRUSTS AND
COUNTERS.
KNOWING ONLY MY OWN CURRENT NEEDS
TO BE GAY, FUN LOVING . . . KEEP IT LIGHT.
SOMETIMES NOT WANTING SERIOUS THROGHTS TO CRUSH
MY TENDER MOOD.
ONLY FEELING THE PRESENT JOY OF ENCOUNTER WITH YOU.
BLEND YOUR MOOD TO MINE WHEN THIS HAPPENS
AND I WILL DO THE SAME FOR YOU.

YOUR BUTTERFLY MIND DRIFTS THRU THE CANYONS
LOOKING FOR A SOFT AND YIELDING PLACE TO STOP AND
DRINK THE NECTAR.
THE MOMENT FOR YOU IS NOW. NOT THE WAS NOR THE
WILL BE, NOR THE CAN BE.
DON'T LOOK OVER YOUR SHOULDER TO THE SHADOWY,
SAD LONELY PLACE OF THOSE WHO CRY FOR YOUR LOVE.
DON'T LOOK INTO THE MISTY TOMORROW THAT
PROMISES, PROMISES, PROMISES.
SAD, BUT YOU MUST RIDE THE WIND, BUTTERFLY MIND.

YOU WOO ME WITH YOUR EYES AND TOUCH ME LIGHTLY
A FRIENDLY EMBRACE, WE FIT TOGETHER NICELY.
MY BREAST AND HIPS FILL THE HILLS AND VALLEYS OF
YOURBODY.
ONE THING HOLDS ME BACK.
YOU ARE OPEN TO THE NOW.
I AM OPEN TO FOREVER.
WE, AS YET, JUST DANCE OUR COURTSHIP
AS TWO BIRDS THAT WISH TO MATE.

The Winepress

Who am I not to forgive the woman too young for Motherhood
Who wanted freedom after birthing three.
Angry for the extra trouble, and wounding tender bodies and minds
With mean whippings and meaner words thrown helter-skelter.
All the memories left to marinate, to ruminate on the bitter tasting wrath.
Yet laying the blame, the shame and the pain at the feet of my protagonist.
Who was I to marry the same, then carry the blame for my own dismal failures?
The heavy hand was not stayed, for the fearful past constrained me.
As tender minds and eyes looked accusingly at me.
The years pass and I have not forgotten the wrongs, but
I also remember the times when I lay my head in my mother's lap, felt her cold hand on my fevered brow.
And now, at long last acknowledging her obvious pride in my grownup accomplishments.
Would I have been the same person if I had not suffered?
Who am I?
We are all in the winepress; grapes, sour and sweet,
Crushed by the weight of our sufferings.
Made wine, set aside to age and perhaps learn patience and forgiveness
Or then again, to tirelessly agitate the grim sediment of old memories that remain inert, except for our introspection.

OUR DEEPEST FEAR IS NOT THAT WE ARE INADEQUATE,

OUR DEEPEST FEAR IS THAT WE ARE POWERFUL BEYOND MEASURE.

IT IS OUR LIGHT, NOT OUR DARKNESS, THAT MOST FRIGHTENS US.

WE ASK OURSELVES, WHO AM I TO BE BRILLIANT, GORGEOUS, TALENTED, FABULOUS?

ACTUALLY, WHO ARE YOU NOT TO BE?

YOU ARE A CHILD OF GOD. YOUR "PLAYING SMALL" DOES NOT SERVE THE WORLD.

THERE IS NOTHING ENLIGHTENING ABOUT SHRINKING SO THAT OTHER PEOPLE WON'T FEEL INSECURE AROUND YOU.

WE WERE BORN TO MAKE MANIFEST THE GLORY OF GOD THAT IS WITHIN US.

IT IS NOT JUST IN SOME OF US; IT IS IN EVERYONE, AND AS WE LET OUR OWN LIGHTS SHINE, WE UNCONSCIOUSLY GIVE OTHER PEOPLE PERMISSION TO DO THE SAME.

AS WE ARE LIBERATED FROM OUR OWN FEAR, OUR OWN PRESENCE AUTOMATICALLY LIBERATES OTHERS.

The Remains

BURY MY BODY DEEP IN THE DELTA WATERS. LET MINE BLEND WITH THE REMEMBRANCES OF THOSE WHO LIVES WERE WEDDED TO THE RIVER.

FISHERMEN AND CAPTAINS OF SHIPS THAT PLYED THE SACRAMENTO'S WINDING MAISE OF WATERWAYS.

YET, LET ME COLLECT THE MEMORIES THAT RISE LIKE FLOTSDAM TO THE SURFACE, RIDING ON THE EFFULGENCE OF INDUSTRIAL EXCRETIONS THATQ MARRED THE CLEAR WATERS . . . UNTIL MEN MUST TURN THEIR BACKS UPON THE WASTE.

OR

TAKE ME TO THE WSPRING GREEN HILLS OF NORTONVILLE, WHERE MINE, AND THE POWDERED BONES OF WORK-WORN COAL MINERS AND FARMERS CAN MINGLE. LET THEIR STORY BE CARRIED ON THE WINDS THAT SWEEP THROUGH THE CANYONS, THEN DRIFT DOWN TO KISS THE EARTH. NO DARK AND DANK GRAVE FOR ME, BUT LET ME BARE MY BREAST TO THE SUBTLE MINDS HUNGRY FOR THE PAST HOLD CLOSE THE WORDS THAT BRIDGE THE PRECEEDANT GENERATIONS.

YOUR BLOOD, YOUR BONE, YOUR HEART IS LIVING STILL IN MY WORDS.

THERE IS A SEASON

TO CREATE AND RECREATE

UNTIL REALITY BITES.

THE SPIRIT HIGH,

YOUR BODY NIGH,

MY HEART DELIGHTS.

THE TEMPERATURE FALLS

THE SEASONS PASS

I'M HOME AT LAST

AND DUTY CALLS

The Temperature Falls.

THE SEASONS PASS

I'M HOME AT LAST
AND DUTY CALLS.

YOU HAVE UNFOLDED ME LIKE A MAP

AND TRACED WITH KNOWING FINGERS
ALL THE ROADS IN ME, THAT LEADS TO YOU.

HOW OFTEN I HAVE LOOKED TO YOU

ALONG THIS WAYWARD PATH OF OURS
AND FOUND YOU THERE BESIDE ME,
SOMEHOW CERTAIN OF THE WAY.

NOW WHEN YOU MAP OUT A PATHWAY

OF YOUR DREAMS AND WANTS,
I CAN TRUST THAT YOU CAN MAKE IT
HAPPEN FOR YOU AND FOR ME.

HELP ME TO REMEMBER YOUR

STEADFASTNESS WHEN I STEP AWAY FROM YOU
AND FEEL UNSURE OF MY DIRECTION.

DRAW ME AS YOU ALWAYS HAVE WITH YOUR TOUCH.

NOW AND FOREVER.

IDEAL, THE LIVING SACRIFICE

Flights of Fancy

THE MERGING OF OUR HEATS DESIRE
THE WE, OF US AND GOD.

OUR BODY AND OUR SPIRIT LAID UPON

HIS ALL CONSUMING LOVE.

POETS ARE PECULIAR PEOLE WHO WEAR MANY HATS.

HE IS A MAGICIAN REACHING INTO HIS BAG OF TRICKS,

SLOWLY PULLING WORDS FROM HIS SIDE POCKET, LIKE

MANY COLORED SCARVES TIED TOGETHER AT THE CORNER

LEAVING A TRAIL OF BRIGHTLY MIXED METAPHORS.

SHE IS A DOCTOR; A SELF-DIAGNOSED HEALER.

WHEN TEMPORARY WOUNDS APPEAR, A SALVE

OF INTERNAL DIALOGUE IS PRESCRIBED
TO HEAL THE INFECTED PLACES THAT ERUPTED.

HE IS A SOLDIER, KILLING ME SOFTLY WITH WORDS.

HIS TONGUE LIKE A SWORD, DEFTLY HANDLED.

SHE IS A CLOWN; PLAY-ACTING WITH A SMILE PAINTED
ONE DROOPING MOUTH; PAN/TOMIMING.
(IT WAS A BEAUTIFUL PERFORMANCE)
LOOK AT THE JUGGLERS: CLEVER WORDS TUMBLING THROUGH
THE AIR. THROWN UP WITH NIMBLE TONGUE,

AND CAUGHT BEFORE HITTING THE FLOOR.

HE IS THE POLICE INSPECTOR; EXAMINING THE SITE

OF AN ATTACT AND MURDER OF THE ENGLISH LANGUAGE. THE
PERPETRATOR WAS CAUGHT, AND WAS FOUND GUILTY OF
PLAGIARIZED WORDS ON THE FIRST COUNT, AND BURYING THE
COPYRIGHT E VIDENCE ON THE 2ND.

POETS ARE ALSO MISERS; CARESSING THE HOARDED WORDS IN THOUGHT CASHES, AND RUNNING THEM THROUGH THE FINGERS OF THEIR MINDS, LIKE COLLECTED COINS.

THE ROOM IS GETTING TOO CROWDED WITH LOQUACIOUS ACTORS IN FUNNY HATS.

I'M OUTTA HERE!

My attempt at exotic cooking was nothing compared to the interesting dishes cooked by my Italian mother-in-law.

AN IRREVERENT SALUTE TO ITALIAN CUISINE

by

Marti Aiello

The following recipes have been carefully guarded by my in-laws and I am boldly endangering my relations with them by passing them on to you, dear reader.

Rezcei (Sea Urchins)

1. Set the speedometer at .0 then go 129 miles

2. Dress warmly at about 75 degree.

3. Approach Italian fisherman with greenbacks in hand. In a low voice, plead your case in the Italian vernacular. Fresh caught and large, make exchange

4. When transaction is complete, return to car. Put on recordings of Louis Prima, followed by Frank Sinatra or Perry Como.

5. Once back in Pittsburg, go directly to the Cardinale house and beg them to make a couple of loaves of French bread.

6. Return home with fresh catch and accompanying bread under arm and receive the accolades you deserve from yo' Mama.

7. Crack the sea urchins open with a knife and enjoy.

Invite everyone to partake of the raw sea urchin's insides that look's like baby poop. Bon appetite!

Babalucci

Collect a large number of garden snails. Place in a cardboard box and cover with a dishtowel. Tack down so that the little rascals don't escape and leave smears all over the kitchen floor. Feed them on bread and water for seven days then boil in a pot for five minutes. The snails can be extracted with a safety pin. Encourage your children who may be sympathizing with the little creatures who they have grown to love, that they are "deliciouso.' Smack your lips and keep repeating, "deliciouso, deliciouso." They won't believe you of course, but try. It also helps to be Italian so that they can understand the word, "deliciouso'. Bon appetite!